HOPE IS A FERRIS WHEEL

a novel by

ROBIN HERRERA

AMULET BOOKS
NEW YORK

HOPE IS A FERRIS WHEEL

PUBLISHER'S NOTE: This is a work of fiction. Names, characters, places, and incidents are either the product of the author's imagination or are used fictitiously, and any resemblance to actual persons, living or dead, business establishments, events, or locales is entirely coincidental.

Library of Congress Cataloging-in-Publication Data

Herrera, Robin.
Hope is a ferris wheel / Robin Herrera.
pages cm
Summary: After moving from Oregon to a trailer park in California, ten-year-old Star participates in a poetry club, where she learns some important lessons about herself and her own hopes and dreams for the future.
ISBN 978-1-4197-1039-1 (alk. paper)
[1. Trailer camps—Fiction. 2. Poetry—Fiction. 3. Clubs—Fiction.] I. Title.
PZ7.H432136Ho 2014
[Fic]—dc23
2013026392

Book design by Maria T. Middleton

Published in 2014 by Amulet Books, an imprint of ABRAMS.

TO MY SISTER, JESSICA:
OLDER, WISER,
INFINITELY COOLER
—R. H.

Amulet Books and Amulet Paperbacks are registered trademarks of Harry N. Abrams, Inc.

Printed and bound in U.S.A.
10 9 8 7 6 5 4 3 2 1

Amulet Books are available at special discounts when purchased in quantity for premiums and promotions as well as fundraising or educational use. Special editions can also be created to specification. For details, contact specialsales@abramsbooks.com or the address below.

ABRAMS
THE ART OF BOOKS SINCE 1949
115 West 18th Street
New York, NY 10011
www.abramsbooks.com

CHAPTER 1

Everyone at Pepperwood Elementary knows that I live in Treasure Trailers, in the pink-tinted trailer with the flamingo hot-glued to the roof. The problem is, I only told four girls, the ones who were standing by me the first time we lined up for recess.

"Isn't that next to the dump?" one of them asked.

"Well, there's a fence," I told them.

The third one behind me scowled and said, "My mom says only drug addicts live there."

"There're no drug addicts," I said. "Well, maybe there're drug addicts. I haven't met everyone yet."

"Hey," said the girl in front of me. She must have overheard. "What's the deal with your hair?"

"Oh, Gloria did it," I said, holding out a strand so she could see the midnight blue streaks. "She went to beauty school. I use anti-frizz. I could get you some," I offered. Gloria gets a good discount from Style Cuts, where she works, and she gets the expired stuff for free. We have tons of anti-frizz in the bathroom and practically every kind of conditioner.

"No thanks," the girl said. "I don't want a mullet."

I heard three distinct giggles behind me. Those three girls were laughing *at* me. I couldn't believe it.

But then I could, the next day, when everyone in class was asking me for anti-frizz. The thing was, they didn't mean it. I mean, boys were asking me for it, and they couldn't even get through the whole question without breaking into giggles. I had to go look up the word *mullet* when everyone started saying that, too.

"It's not a mullet," I told Winter, the day I found out what one was. "Mullets are flat and ugly."

Winter sat me down at our built-in table and combed her fingers through my hair. My hair's so thick, though, that I could hardly even feel it. "It's because of all the different lengths," Winter said. "It's all short here and long here, so—"

"It's a *layered cut*. That's what Gloria called it. Why does everyone think it's a mullet?"

Shrugging, Winter headed to the fridge. "I mean, it's not like you told them you live in a trailer park," she said, passing me a couple of oranges to peel.

"Of course I did."

"Star!" Winter said as she slammed the fridge door shut. "You did not say that."

"But—but—what about in Oregon?" I asked. "No one said I had a mullet there! And no one cared that I lived in a trailer park."

"Yeah, because half the kids at school were from the trailer park! Haven't you noticed anything different about California, Star?"

Yes, I had. There were no other kids at Treasure Trailers. There were a couple of babies and a million cats, but there was nobody even close to my age.

"You're probably the only kid at school who lives in a trailer park," Winter went on. "And everyone thinks trailer parks are full of gross people."

I sighed, remembering what that girl's mom had said. Was that what everyone thought? I started peeling the first orange. Winter peels them off in one long piece, but I haven't been able to do that yet. I can only do it with mandarins. "So is that why they call me Star Trashy? Because we're next to the dump?"

"It's because we're trailer trash, Star," Winter said, taking the elastic out of her hair. "And *Trashy* kind of rhymes with *Mackie*." She shook her head, and all her lovely black curls tumbled down past her shoulders.

It's too bad my hair isn't curly like hers—no one would think I had a mullet then. But I got Mom's thick, straight hair that never needs volumizer. The only good thing about it is that it's naturally black. Winter has to use dye.

"Do they call you Winter Trashy at Sarah Borne?"

"No. You know why? Because no one knows I live in a trailer park." She plucked the orange out of my hand and had it peeled in ten seconds flat. "Anyway, even if they did, I doubt they'd make fun of me that much. There're plenty of other delinquents to pick on. The pregnant girls get teased the most."

"You're not a delinquent," I said.

"Yes, but I still go to delinquent school," she said, and she started working on the second orange. I asked if they were going to let her take a creative writing class this semester, but she just scoffed, shaking her head. "They had to cancel the class. They were three students short of the minimum."

That was too bad. I knew how much Winter wanted to take that class. It was the only thing she'd been looking forward to once Mom told her she couldn't go back to public school yet. The worst thing was, they wouldn't even let her start a new club, considering how the last one had turned out.

"Hey," I said. "Maybe I could start a club."

"Hey!" Winter repeated. "Just don't do a writing club, or Mom will burst a blood vessel."

"I won't. I'll think of something else." I split the oranges into segments and divided them between us. They were a little old and a little dry, and Mom had accidentally picked up the seeded kind, so we had to spit our seeds out onto the table.

"I guess it'd be a good way to make friends," Winter said. "I mean, I don't talk to anyone from my old writing club anymore, but . . ." Frowning, she flicked an orange seed onto the linoleum. "I'm sure *you* won't get yourself expelled."

I told her I wouldn't. "I have to think of something good, though. A club everyone will want to join. Then they'd have to be my friends, or I won't let them in!" I pictured everyone's faces and their clasped hands as they pleaded with me. As long as they were really sincere, I'd think about letting them join. "What do you think—" I started to ask Winter, but I was interrupted by the slam of a car door outside.

That was the end of our conversation. Winter raced to the top bunk with her backpack and kicked her combat boots off the side. A few seconds later Mom walked in, loaded down with groceries, followed by Gloria, still in her Style Cuts apron. "Heavenly Donuts!" Gloria yelled, loudly enough for the whole trailer park to hear. "I don't remember it being this cold in Oregon!"

"Hey, Star, put these away, will you?" was the only thing Mom said to me before she noticed Winter. "I can see you sulking there, Winter," she said, which I thought was pretty obvious—you can see every inch of the trailer from the front door, except for Mom's room, which Winter wouldn't be in anyway. "How was school today?"

And just like every day since the end of summer, Winter said nothing.

Mom straightened her glasses and said, "I just don't get it," before pulling a pizza out of the freezer. I got it, but I was busy putting the groceries away, and when I finally finished, Mom and Gloria were already talking about some woman who'd only tipped Gloria a dollar on a dye job. When I asked if that was bad, they both scoffed and threw their hands up in the air, so I decided to just stay quiet for the rest of the night.

CHAPTER 2

I spend a lot of time at school staring at the back of Denny Libra's head, wishing I had superpowers so my eyes could bore a hole right between his ears and see what Mr. Savage is writing on the whiteboard.

But it's not like Denny doesn't do the same thing to me when he turns around to pass papers back; he glares at my forehead like he's trying to vaporize it. I'm sure he'd rather look at Delilah Manning, who sits behind me, but is it my fault that Mr. Savage made all the fifth-graders sit alphabetically?

Today was different, though. Staring into the void of Denny's black hair, I finally came up with the perfect idea for a club. Mr. Savage was busy telling us about our vocabulary words, but I already knew what he wanted, so I turned my notebook to a fresh piece of paper and wrote, **The Trailer Park Club**.

It was absolutely perfect. I could teach our members about all the good things in trailer parks so that they'd stop thinking trailer parks were full of trash. (Although, with our flamingo-capped trailer being right next to the dump, sometimes trash just finds its way over the fence.) Maybe I could even figure out a way to talk about layered haircuts and how they are not mullets at all.

After school I asked Mr. Savage if I could hang a sign for my new club in the classroom. This was something I'd learned from Winter: if you're asking for something, make sure you sound like you already have it.

Mr. Savage rubbed his beard for a few seconds and then asked, "You want to start a club? No one's ever wanted to start a club." Mr. Savage has only been a teacher for two years, but I couldn't believe he'd never had anyone ask about clubs before. "You want to have it here?"

"At the school? Yes," I said.

"In my classroom," he said, now scratching his beard.

"Yeah."

"You want me to supervise it?"

"I don't need a supervisor," I told him. "If you leave me the key, I'll lock up when I'm done." I used to do this for my third-grade teacher in Oregon so she could get to her second job on time. "I can leave the key in the drainpipe for you," I added, pointing out the window.

"You know, I prefer to lock my own classroom." The scratching increased, and behind my back, I crossed my fingers for luck. "I stay late on Wednesdays. Can you do Wednesdays?"

Wednesdays would be fine, but Winter says that you should always act like the first offer isn't good enough, so I pretended to think about it, scratching my own chin and looking at the ceiling. After I counted to six in my head, I said, "I guess that'll work."

Mr. Savage went back to his computer, and I thought about asking if I could use it to make some posters. But Winter says you can't ask for too much too soon, and she's the club expert.

So I headed home. Maybe Winter had some of her old club flyers left, and maybe Mom would let me use the white-out she took from her last temp job so I could make some updates. Instead of THE CREATIVE WRITING CLUB, it'd say THE TRAILER PARK CLUB, maybe with a picture of a clean-looking trailer. And below that: NOW OPEN FOR MEMBERSHIP.

CHAPTER 3

The pickup truck was in the driveway when I got to Treasure Trailers, which marked the first time in months that Winter had beaten me home. She was supposed to have lots of extra work to do after school, since she'd missed half her sophomore year in Oregon, but maybe she'd gotten it all done already. Maybe now that real school had started, she could be around more often.

I pulled open the doors and announced, "Hey, Winter! I started a Trailer Park Club!" But then my eyes adjusted to the darkness, and I saw that I was talking to an empty trailer. I checked the driveway again to make sure I hadn't been seeing things, but, yup, the truck was still sitting there, empty cab and all. The trailer was truly empty, too—

Winter wasn't in the bathroom or in the closet or even in her bed. Slamming the screen door shut behind me, I climbed into Winter's truck—she never locks the doors—and opened up the glove box.

It was stuffed with Winter's stories, all folded into thick, tiny squares. A couple of them were typed, probably at the library or at school, but most she'd written in red pen. My favorite one wasn't even in there—maybe her old principal still had it, if he hadn't thrown it away or burned it or given it to the police.

Mom said I wasn't allowed to read Winter's stories anymore, since the characters in them have the misfortune of dying horrible deaths, like having all the blood explode out of their bodies. My favorite story was about Winter axing a bunch of zombies who were trying to eat her brain. She'd tried telling the principal that she was going to change the names later, since some of the zombies just happened to have the same names as some of her classmates, but I guess everyone had been freaking out, especially after they'd read Winter's novella about the family of inbred mutant cannibals.

I don't think Winter should have been expelled at all, especially over a story, but the school board didn't agree. They wanted Winter to go to counseling, which we couldn't pay for, so Mom decided we should just move instead and find a new school for Winter. We left as soon as Gloria got her beauty school diploma in June.

So all of Winter's best stories were gone now, but she still had lots of others hidden away. I unfolded a good one called "Hand It to You," about this girl's amputated hand trying to reattach itself to her arm every night. The ending always makes me laugh.

About three stories later, a knock on the driver's-side window nearly made me scream. It was Winter, wearing her giant sunglasses and carrying a plastic dollar-store bag. "What'd you get?" I asked, when she opened the door and climbed in.

"Buncha candy," she said, handing me a box of gummy bears. "Don't let Mom see these." And she stuffed her tiny story squares back into the glove box. "She'd probably make me do an extra semester at Sarah Borne if she found out. I've gotta get out of that place." Her head sagged, and she held it in both hands as if, if she didn't, it'd fall into her lap.

"You will," I said, and as I reached out to put my hand on her shoulder, she started to cry. I couldn't even remember the last time I'd seen Winter cry. She hadn't shed a single tear when she got expelled, or even when Mom took away the card Dad had sent her for her thirteenth birthday. All the times I'd ever cried, Winter had held my hand or put her chin on my head and told me not to worry, that things would get better. So I did that—put my hand on Winter's. "It's okay," I said.

But it wasn't okay, and it didn't help at all. Winter sat there sobbing, and I had nothing to say. I thought I could tell her about my club, but would that cheer her up, or would it make things even worse? Maybe it would remind Winter that she wasn't allowed to form clubs anymore.

So I didn't say anything, just kept my hand there, and eventually Winter's huge shuddering breaths turned into soft sniffles. "It's okay," she said, even though I wasn't the one crying. "I'm just . . . tired of being at that school. I'm tired of feeling like a loser."

"You're not a loser," I told her. "You're the coolest person I know!" She lifted her head the tiniest bit, so I fired off a couple more compliments. "You're a really good writer, and your makeup's always perfect, and . . . and . . ." I reached deep into my mind for something really, really good. "And Dad sent you a birthday card."

She swiveled her head, and I saw my face reflected in her glasses. "Three years ago," she said. "Geez, I almost forgot about that. Whatever—it wasn't that big of a deal."

"He never sent *me* a card," I pointed out.

"Mom probably wouldn't let him." Shifting, Winter moved her hand so that it folded around mine. With her other hand, she took off her sunglasses and wiped away the stray tears on her cheeks, smudging her eyeliner. "She doesn't even let him pay child support, which is just stupid."

"I know," I said. My hand felt warm and safe inside Winter's. "But he *did* send you a card, even though he wasn't supposed to. And he *did* give you the truck, when he could have just given it to Mom. Doesn't that mean something?"

The cab was silent for several minutes. Mrs. O'Grady came out of her trailer with a sagging trash bag and jumped when she saw us just sitting there inside the truck. She crept back into her trailer, taking her bag with her.

"There was a note at the bottom of the card," Winter said. "Right before he signed his name. He said, 'Hope you and your sister are doing well.'" She squeezed my hand. "Do you think *that* means something?"

"He really said that?"

"Yup."

"Really?"

"Yup."

Heavenly Donuts! Mom was always saying Dad didn't really care about us, that he was a nice man deep down but a very terrible father. That he would never be there for us when we really needed him, which was why it was better if he didn't contact us at all.

But maybe that one little line proved that he cared, even if it was just the tiniest bit.

I wished I could hold that card in my hands to see the way he'd written it. Sloppily? Carefully? In slanting cursive that was hard to read?

If he'd gone through all that trouble to send Winter a card, it wasn't so hard to believe he'd send me one someday. Maybe he was waiting until I turned thirteen, too. In that case, I'd only have to wait three more years.

Winter and I stayed in the cab even after it started to get dark. I didn't get to work on my club flyers, but Winter helped me with all my vocabulary words, so I didn't have to lug out the dictionary.

It was nice to know that the club was going so well. I mean, the hardest part was being allowed to start it, and that was already done. The flyers would be easy, and once everyone saw them, they'd join in a snip.

I just wished Winter's problems would go away that easily, too.

Star Mackie

September 18

Week 1 Vocabulary Sentences

ABUNDANT. Like, lots of. Where I live, there are a lot of cats, like tumbleweeds in a desert, except here cats tumble around under your feet. Unlike tumbleweeds, cats make yowling sounds when you step on them. That is one of the many differences between cats and tumbleweeds.

ALTERNATIVE. This means a choice. Another choice. My sister goes to an alternative high school now, and it's full of shoplifters and juvenile delinquents and pregnant girls. Alternative sounds like a choice, but it doesn't seem like she had much of a choice to me. The juvies probably didn't have a choice either.

CIRCUMSTANTIAL. Sometimes we watch Crime TV, and that is where I hear this word the most, and it's always followed by "evidence." I think it means that it makes someone look guilty but doesn't actually prove anything, so it's like how Mom and Gloria are always calling Dad a deadbeat jerk, but since I've never met him, I don't know if that's really true.

COVERT. Hidden, like a secret, or a spy. If I were a

spy, I would want to be covert and not attract attention to myself, but I guess I'm not cut out to be a spy, because I already attracted attention to myself with my layered blue haircut. Most fifth-graders don't have layered cuts or blue hair, but they are also not spies.

HYSTERICAL. This is my favorite. It means funny but also crazy. On the first day of school I heard some kids talking about Mrs. Feinstein, who's this fourth-grade teacher (you probably know her, Mr. Savage) who worked in a canning factory in college, and one day—FWOOMP!—off went her pinkie, because it was too close to one of the cutters. Now she keeps it in a jar in her desk, everyone says, and sometimes she takes it out and waves it around at her students when they aren't paying attention, and she says, "SEE WHAT HAPPENS WHEN YOU DON'T PAY ATTENTION?" Which is funny when you hear it from fourth-graders but probably not so funny when you're sitting in the front row of Mrs. Feinstein's class.

LANKY. I made a memory booster for this word. We had memory boosters at my old school, where you take each letter of the word and make it mean something different. So for LANKY it's Long As Nine Knobby Yardsticks. I know the Knobby part doesn't make sense, but I was thinking knobby like knees, because lanky people are usually skinny-legged, and their knees stick out, like Denny's (you know him, Mr. Savage, because he sits right in front of me). Do you ever notice how far out of his desk his legs stick? I have noticed.

NEUTRAL. I asked my sister what this meant, and she said Switzerland, which makes no sense. Then she said it's when you don't pick a side, and sometimes that can be worse than picking the wrong side. Like in our home lately, there is my mom's side and my sister's side. I try to not be on any side, but secretly I'm always on my sister's side. Things aren't always her fault like Mom says.

POVERTY. I think people associate this with trailer parks, because they think, "Those people are too poor to afford a real house." I guess that's pretty much the meat of it, but I think there's a difference between when my mom says why we live in a trailer park and when everyone else says why we live in a trailer park.

RELUCTANT. When you are reluctant, it means you don't want to do something. I didn't want to leave Oregon, especially because in California you have to pay sales tax on everything. You wouldn't think eight percent is that big a deal, but it makes a pretty big difference when you buy something for $3.99, and you only have four dollars, and—surprise!—sales tax.

VEXATION. No one uses this word, ever, Mr. Savage.

I know what it means, but I'm never going to use it, because it's a pretty old word. I'm just telling you for your own good that no one ever says vexation unless they are about a hundred years old.

CHAPTER 4

So, I did not turn in my vocabulary sentences. Everyone else did, but I didn't, because I got the directions a hundred percent wrong.

We were supposed to use the word in a sentence. *We were supposed to* use the word *in a sentence*. Not a thousand sentences, the way I did. And most of my sentences didn't even use the words!

I almost turned the homework in before I realized my mistake, but luckily Mr. Savage collected all the papers alphabetically (like our seating) and started with the fourth-graders before moving on to the fifth-graders. There are only eight fourth-graders, and they usually have different homework assignments, but we all have the same vocabulary words. I've never been in a class with two grades in it, but Pepperwood has a bunch of them.

Meg Anderson was first, so I had time to look over Denny's shoulder to check out what he'd written, and I noticed that, first of all, he'd numbered all his sentences, and, second of all, each sentence was just that, one sentence, and third, the vocabulary words were underlined, and fourth, he had only used one sheet of paper instead of four.

I bet even the teachers at Sarah Borne wouldn't have accepted my homework. They would have laughed and laughed and marked it with a big red check-minus. (Winter says the teachers can't give out grades there.)

By the time Mr. Savage got to me, I had already crumpled up my four vocabulary pages and shoved them deep into my desk. I told him I'd left my paper at home, and he said, "Okay, just bring it next time, then." After he walked away, a drop of sweat slithered its way down the back of my neck, and I was glad that at least some parts of my hair were long enough to hide it.

When recess started, I snuck over to the trash can by the door and threw my sentences away. Denny Libra glared at me the whole time and didn't stop until I left the room.

I was so upset, I could only think of one word to describe how I felt.

Vexation.

CHAPTER 5

On Thursday night Mom made macaroni bake, the best thing she cooks. It's macaroni and cheese, plus sliced-up hot dogs and bell peppers, with bread crumbs baked on top. We used the nice plates, and Gloria lit a candle and set it on the built-in table, and we all sat down to eat.

Winter shuffled the noodles around on her plate, not saying anything, as usual, until she uncovered a bit of hot dog. Then she pushed her plate away, folded her arms, and said, "I'm a vegetarian."

Gloria dropped her fork. This was the first time Winter had spoken in front of Mom for nearly a month. Only Mom was unsurprised and kept eating like nothing weird was going on. All she said was, "Eat your food, Winter."

Winter pushed her plate farther across the table, knocking over the saltshaker. "I don't eat meat anymore. I find it vile."

"Well, that would have been nice to know an hour ago, when I was cooking it," Mom said. "And I don't recall anyone putting in a request for fancy tofu dogs when we still had money on the food card."

"I don't eat meat," Winter said again, and she crossed her arms.

Gloria grimaced, which she is very good at. Usually it's funny to see a frown stretch across her face, but this time no one laughed. "Well, then," she said to Mom, picking up her plate, "see you tomorrow, Carly." And she left.

Once the door closed, Mom said to Winter, "Fine. But I'm not going to see good food wasted in this house." She started picking out all the hot dog slices with her fingers and putting them on my plate, and even though I like hot dogs, my stomach cramped. I wondered why Winter hadn't told me anything about being a vegetarian.

Once Mom was finished, Winter took a bite of the macaroni noodles, letting some of the cheese drip off first. "Ugh. I can still taste the meat."

"Well, next time, Winter, I will know that I have to read your mind before I start dinner," Mom said, her eyes narrowing and shrinking to the size of raisins. "Besides, hot dogs aren't even real meat."

I almost choked on the hot dog I had just swallowed.

"I'm gonna eat some cottage cheese," Winter said, scooting past me. A few seconds later I heard her say, from the fridge, "Great. It's expired."

"It just expired yesterday," Mom said. "And it's not even really expired—that's just a best-by date. You'll be fine. I can't count the number of times I've fed you girls 'expired' cheese."

I almost choked on the macaroni I'd just swallowed.

Winter came back to the table juggling the tub of cottage cheese, a spoon, and a package of English muffins. I scooted over so she wouldn't have to climb over me, but that meant Winter and Mom were now sitting right across from each other. Aside from the crinkling of plastic coming from Winter opening up the muffins, and the clatter of Mom's fork against her plate, the trailer was silent.

"Um," I said, wanting to change the subject, and Mom and Winter both looked at me. "What does Dad do?"

Mom's eyes shrank even more. Talking about Dad is pretty much forbidden in the trailer. Or in front of Mom at all. Or even in front of Gloria, who will run and tell Mom instantly that her daughters are starting to get curious about their bloodline. "Don't call him *Dad*. If you have to call him anything, call him your . . . your genetic donor."

"What does our genetic donor do?" I asked, which made Winter snort.

Across the table, Mom's shoulders hunched and she shrank into herself. The angrier she is, the smaller she gets. "He doesn't *do* anything, Star. He isn't fit to be a father."

"I mean, what's his job?" I asked as Mom shrank down still farther in her seat. I'd probably gone too far now, but I'd been wondering about Dad even more since Winter told me about the line on the birthday card. "Where does he work?"

Winter jumped right in. "What's his favorite hobby? How much money does he make? How old is he?" We already knew the answer to the last one because Gloria let it slip once, but Mom had reached her shrinking limit. She grabbed all the food and plates from the table and threw them in the sink.

"Go to bed, both of you. If I hear one more word about *that man*, you'll both be grounded. GO!"

Winter left, her combat boots stomping along the linoleum. I got our toothbrushes and changed into my pajamas, and the whole time Mom hunched over the sink, staring at the dishes full of food. I wanted to tell her I was sorry for bringing up Dad, but I didn't want her getting any smaller than she already was.

Winter didn't answer when I said good night, which made it hard to fall asleep, knowing she was mad, too.

After a while, I heard Mom's footsteps creak across the trailer to her own bedroom. I stayed awake long after her light turned off, and long after her breathing slowed to a heavy wheeze. From the way Winter's mattress shifted above me, I knew I wasn't the only one awake.

CHAPTER 6

Before the bell rang on Friday, Mr. Savage made an announcement to everyone. "Star is starting a club," he said, holding his arm out to me. I stood up and waved a little bit. "It meets after school on Wednesdays, in this room," he went on. "Star, why don't you tell everyone about your club? What's it called?"

I cleared my throat and said, "It's called the Trailer Park Club."

Someone coughed. It was one of the fourth-graders, I'm sure, because the eight of them sit in their own cluster by the door. I knew I should have run the name by Winter before announcing it.

Mr. Savage had his eyebrows halfway up his forehead.

"The Trailer Park Club?" he asked, and I could tell that he was embarrassed just to say it.

"Yes," I said, "but even if you don't live in a trailer park, you can still come."

Behind me, someone snorted. Well, maybe I wouldn't let them join at all. I sat back down and heard people whispering all around. Pretending not to notice, I pulled out a piece of paper and started working on a flyer, with 3-D block letters that Winter had taught me how to make. I only got to TRA before the bell rang, since block letters are sort of time-consuming.

"Star," Mr. Savage said as everyone left the room, "may I speak with you for a second?"

On the fourth-grade end of the room, Jenny Withagee lingered, stuffing papers into her purple backpack and glancing at me every other second. I skip-walked over to Mr. Savage's desk, where he stood, his hands palms-down on his desk calendar.

"I think your club name may be a little off-putting," he told me. "Maybe if you changed it to something else . . ."

I didn't want to change the name. And I wished Mr. Savage would stop scratching his beard, which he was doing now; it made my face itch. I said nothing—another Winter tactic. She said it put the other person on the defensive, making them scramble for stuff to say, and then they looked so stupid that they just gave up.

"I just don't know if anyone's going to want to join," Mr. Savage said, and he didn't look stupid at all. He looked kind of sad . . . or like he was sad *for me*, which was even worse. I was about to abandon the whole silence plan and start pleading, when an airy voice called out, "I'll be there!"

Jenny appeared next to me, grinning so hard her eyes almost disappeared. I was on the verge of saying, "Fifth-graders only." Not because Jenny wears skirts to her ankles and has rub-on tattoos up and down her arms, which I don't even care about, but because I don't really know who she is, and I had this feeling that she wanted me to be happy that she'd just saved me from having my club taken away, even though she hadn't.

Then I saw Mr. Savage's face. I had no idea his eyebrows could go that high, but I was more angry at him for being so surprised than I was at Jenny for trying to be all heroic.

"See?" I told Mr. Savage. "One member already."

He apologized and said that *of course* I didn't have to change the name, and *of course* the Trailer Park Club was an excellent name. I smiled and walked out the door, glad that my club was saved but unglad that Jenny's footsteps were following mine.

"So," she said, once we were outside in the outdoor hallway, dodging the few other kids who'd gotten out a bit late, "it's on Wednesday? Should I bring anything?" Which bothered me, because I hadn't even thought about bringing stuff myself. But I was saved from answering by, of all people, Denny Libra, who came out from behind one of the cement pillars holding up the hallway roof and curled his fingers around Jenny's tattooed arm.

"Let's go," he said, and he started pulling her away, toward the playground. It was pretty obvious from the glare he was shooting me that he didn't want her talking to me, which I thought was kind of creepy. I grabbed Jenny's other arm and pulled her back, saying, "We're talking about club stuff, donut-brain."

"She's not joining your club!" Denny shouted, so loudly that I had to let go. "You're not joining her club," Denny said to her, and he dragged her away, and she didn't say anything, not one thing; she just followed him onto the blacktop.

I glanced back into the classroom to make sure Mr. Savage hadn't seen, because I wasn't sure he'd let me have my club if he knew the only member had just been yanked right out of it.

CHAPTER 7

The first chance I got to talk to Winter alone since the world's worst vocabulary sentences was on Saturday. Mom said she had a score to settle with the Food Bank, which meant she'd lost her card again and would have to argue a bag of food out of them. Gloria had a bunch of appointments booked, but she'd stopped by that morning to heat up a donut sandwich in our microwave. (Her microwave is haunted.)

When they were both gone, Winter told me she was going to the library.

"Can I go?" I asked.

She was still getting her coat and brushing on eye shadow, so she didn't answer. Not until she put on her giant sunglasses. Then she said, "Are you coming or not?" And luckily I was already dressed.

In the truck, Winter tried to find a decent radio station, but she gave up when she almost hit Mrs. O'Grady's trash cans. Besides, ever since the antenna fell off, the truck's reception isn't great.

"Why are we going to the library?" I asked.

"I need to look something up on the Internet," Winter said.

We used to have a computer and Internet, but the computer died, and then Mom said we didn't need the Internet anyway. Winter kept telling Mom that we needed a new computer so that she could type up her schoolwork, and Mom kept saying she'd put it on the list, right below dental insurance.

Then one day Winter mentioned computers again, and Mom's eyes shrank to raisin size, and she said, "If you want a computer so bad, sell the truck." Mom would love that, but the pickup belongs to Winter. Dad had given it to her right after I was born, before Winter could even drive. It was a few months before he got married to someone else, Gloria told me later. I think it was an apology present because we weren't invited to the wedding.

So Winter would never sell it, even to get twenty computers, and now we use the computers at the library.

They give you a whole designated hour all to yourself, but there's usually a long list of names to wait behind. Luckily, when we got there, the sign-up sheet only had one name that hadn't been crossed off yet.

"Where do you want me to find you?" Winter asked. I couldn't tell where she was looking because of the sunglasses, but I knew she wasn't looking at me.

"I'll be in nonfiction," I said. "I need to read about clubs." Winter didn't say anything, so I added, "I started a club at school," not sure if I'd told her yet.

"A club? Oh, right, so they'll stop with the mullet jokes." Then she adjusted her sunglasses and said, "Why is it so bright in here?" before racing off to the bathroom.

So I wandered around the nonfiction section, looking for club books. I was hoping a title would pop right off the shelf, something like *Clubs for Fun and Profit!* Or, even better: *How to Get Everyone in School to Join Your Club!*

But this library doesn't have exciting books like that, just boring ones about bird-watching and lighthouses. When I hit the seventeenth aisle, I wondered if maybe I should go find one of the catalog computers and make sure this library even *had* books about clubs.

Discouraged, I went back to find Winter. She'd finally gotten on one of the computers, but when I came up behind her, she closed the browser she was looking at.

"No books on clubs?" she guessed. "Well, go upstairs and see if there're any decent movies. Something from after 1980, if possible."

"What kind?" I asked. "Comedy? Romance? Adventure? Zombies?"

"Whatever," she said. "I don't really care. Nothing matters anymore."

The word *why* was on its way out of my mouth, but Winter was already back to the computer, so I trudged up the stairs, wishing Winter wasn't so miserable. Heavenly Donuts! Was it really that bad at Sarah Borne? She'd never complained much in the summer, but I guess in the summer she hadn't thought she'd need to stay that long. I hoped she didn't have to finish high school there.

Besides, now that the school year had started up, there were probably ten times as many delinquents running around at Sarah Borne. Pregnant girls snapping gum in the hallways. Girls with bald spots where chunks of their hair had been pulled out during a fight. Boys with long hair and eyelid piercings.

And she wasn't allowed to have her writing club. Even if she was, who would join? She said most of the kids there didn't even know how to write.

In the movie room I picked out *A League of Their Own*, which is about a pair of sisters, although these two are not at all like Winter and me, because they're constantly fighting over who's better at baseball. Winter told me it was a good choice, but when we were watching it that night, she left halfway through to go to bed.

I wanted to tell Mom that she should maybe consider putting Winter back into public school, but she was already shrunken from dealing with the Food Bank, and without Gloria there to calm her down, I knew it was a lost cause.

CHAPTER 8

When I got to school on Monday, I wasn't even thinking about clubs until Jared Barrel asked if he could join the Trailer Park Club while we were lining up outside Mr. Savage's room. "Sure!" I said, kind of excited, but then he and a bunch of other boys laughed, so I don't think he was serious.

All through class, Denny glared at me like it was his official classroom job. And instead of passing papers back to me, he whammed them onto my desk, making me jump every time his palm hit the polished wood. I think he was trying to scare me, but he's too lanky to be scary.

At recess, I was hanging out on the bench by Mr. Savage's room—where Pepperwood has a map of the United

States painted on the blacktop—when Jenny, grinning, and Denny, glaring, walked up to me.

"I talked to Mom," Jenny informed me, "and she said I could join any club I want." She stopped, maybe waiting for Denny to argue, but he just stood there and did his thing. And then she smiled, said, "See you Wednesday!" and turned and skipped off, her skirt bouncing at her heels. Denny stayed where he was and tried to glare me off the bench.

"Yes?" I asked him.

He left without a word.

But now something was bothering me. Denny and Jenny had some weird thing going on with each other. I thought maybe they were related, except that Jenny's last name was Withagee, and Denny's was Libra.

The roll sheet was already gone by the time we came in for lunch, but Mr. Savage kept a list of all our names—in alphabetical order, which must be his most favorite thing ever—above the pencil sharpener. I pressed my pencil hard against my paper during our practice spelling test so I'd have an excuse to go study the list and make sure I wasn't wrong about Jenny's name, even though I'd heard her clearly the first day of school saying that she was Jenny Withagee.

As it turns out, I was dead wrong, because there wasn't

a single Jenny on that list, not even a Jennifer. But right below Denny Libra was the name Geneva Libra, and it was only after staring at it for a minute that I finally got it.

Jenny *Withagee*. Jenny *with a* G. Genny. Geneva Libra.

Of course.

Then Mr. Savage asked what was taking me so long at that pencil sharpener and had I even sharpened my pencil yet, and so I sharpened my pencil for something like half a second before sitting down again and writing out the next word with a stubby pencil lead. Which I hate.

After school I hung up the very first club flyer in Mr. Savage's room. It had everything: 3-D block letters, glitter, and a picture of a very fancy-looking trailer I'd printed off the Internet.

Hopefully people would see it and decide to join, because there was no way I'd run a club with Denny's sister as the only member.

CHAPTER 9

Winter was acting weirder than ever. She'd sleep in, then get up and not even shower and put on clothes that were lying on the floor, clothes that didn't even go together. Then she'd come home late, with droopy eyes, and half the time she'd say a couple of words, but the other half she'd just head straight to bed.

I started recording Winter's behavior in my club notebook, since I wasn't doing so great a job of putting club stuff in there. The first page had a list of pros and cons about trailer parks, most of which I'd gotten from other people:

Pros	Cons
• Cheap rent (Mom)	• Have to keep stuff in storage (Winter)
• Donut shop down the block, even better than Heavenly Donuts (Gloria)	• Hate walking and driving on gravel (Winter)
• Christmas lights up all year long, looks pretty at night (me)	• Lots of weird neighbors (Winter)

I never finished, though; I was going to ask Mrs. O'Grady when she was in one of her good moods, and slip a note to the guy in the tinfoil-covered trailer who lives next to Gloria, but that never happened. I just flipped my pros-and-cons page and started a new page all about Winter.

She was still vegetarian, but I could tell sometimes she didn't like it, like when Gloria would come over to heat bacon in the microwave and the whole trailer would smell so, so good that I'd beg Gloria to break me off a piece. The only thing better than the smell of bacon is the taste, and I knew Winter hated being able to smell it and not taste it.

Another thing that seemed weird: Winter was letting her roots grow out. She has blond roots, which are extremely noticeable when you dye your hair black. That's not a problem with my hair, because midnight blue and black are both dark colors, but Winter has to dye her hair every month or it looks bad.

Also, I never saw Winter doing homework. But I thought, maybe that's why she was out so late—she was doing homework. Just not at home.

I filled pages and pages with observations, which I knew would have impressed my second-grade teacher, who had made us study worms. My plan was to show Mom the notes and hope she was equally impressed. Then she'd realize that she had to pull Winter out of Sarah Borne once and for all.

Unfortunately, it kind of took away from my club-planning time, so when the Trailer Park Club met for the very first time on Wednesday, at 3:05 in Mr. Savage's room, I was a little unprepared.

But it turned out that didn't matter at all, because despite the extra flyers I'd put up in the outside hallway and on the door and next to the bookcase, the only kids who showed up were Genny and Denny Libra. And I'm pretty sure Denny was only there because he didn't want Genny to be the only member.

"You want to take the minutes?" I asked him, but he just glared back at me, so I decided I'd probably be better at the minutes taking.

3:05 Meeting started

3:06 Denny did not want to take minutes

3:07 I introduced myself

3:08 Genny said I don't think you have to record every minute

3:09 Silence

Then Genny took the minutes from me and said she'd do them, which was good, because I couldn't talk and do minutes at the same time. In the corner, at his desk, Mr. Savage gave a small cough. He was grading papers, I think, and not really paying attention to the meeting.

"So," I said, "this is a club about trailer parks."

Denny rolled his eyes, and I couldn't blame him. Even I knew this was a horrible start. Genny scribbled something in the notes and asked, "Are we ever going to take a field trip to the trailer park?"

I hadn't thought about that, but Denny said, "No," so I said, "Yes," much louder. "But not until another meeting."

On the minutes Genny wrote, *Field Trip TBA*. Then she asked, "What's Treasure Trailers like?"

"I made a list of pros and cons!" I'd only just remembered that, so I dug the notebook out of my backpack and opened it to the first page.

"Donuts is a pro?" Genny asked after half a minute.

"That's from Gloria," I explained. "She's like my godmother, because she and my mom are best friends. We used to eat at this place called Heavenly Donuts in Oregon." I was so busy talking, I didn't even notice that Denny was writing on my list. "Hey!" I snatched it away and read what he'd written in the cons column: *Next to the dump*.

"It's separated by a very high chain-link fence with barbed wire and everything," I told him. "It's not like we have junk lying all over the place." Which was kind of a lie, because the trailer across from ours had rusted lawn chairs scattered in front of it, and even though Mrs. O'Grady had put up portable fencing around her trailer, I'd seen filled-to-the-brim trash bags piled in her designated driveway.

The rest of the meeting went flaming down a cliff from there. Every time Genny asked a question, Denny tried to answer it before me, and his answers were completely untrue. He said the reason we leave Christmas lights up all year long is because we're too lazy to take them down, and that everyone in the trailer park lives off welfare.

"Not the tinfoil guy!" I corrected him. "He doesn't trust the government, so he doesn't take anything from them!"

To make matters worse, Genny recorded everything we said in the minutes.

After an hour Mr. Savage kicked us out, saying that he

wanted to go home. I again offered to lock the classroom and leave the keys in the drainpipe, but Mr. Savage didn't even answer, and within a few minutes we found ourselves outside, in the hallway, watching the rain splatter against the cement. Mr. Savage was gone in another minute, whipping out his umbrella and reminding me about my vocabulary sentences, which I hadn't even done yet, before he headed out to the parking lot.

For a while, the only sound came from the rain hitting the roof of the hallway. To break the silence, I said, "I like your tattoos," to Genny.

"Thanks!" she said. "They were a gift from our brother's girlfriend."

It made me sad to think there was another Denny running around, and sadder to think there was some poor girl *dating* the other Denny.

"I'm gonna get a real one someday," Genny said. "I don't know what, but I want it to cover my whole back. And then I want—"

"You're not getting any tattoos," Denny said, and without saying good-bye, he grabbed his sister's arm and dragged her away. Genny waved back at me with her other hand and said, "See you tomorrow!"

"See you," I said. It was too bad, because Genny was really nice. She just had the misfortune of having the world's worst brother. But Genny's being nice was not going to keep everyone from teasing me about my stupid mull—*layered cut*.

The wind picked up, taking down a corner of the flyer I'd taped to the outside of Mr. Savage's door. I went ahead and ripped the whole thing down to save the wind the trouble.

Maybe if I canceled the club now, no one would remember that I'd ever tried to start it in the first place.

CHAPTER 10

That night, before Winter came home, I asked Mom if she'd ever let me get a tattoo.

"Sure," she said, "but you have to let me draw it." This was a joke, I could tell, because Mom can't even draw stick figures. "Why?" she asked. "Does Winter have a tattoo I don't know about?"

Winter didn't have any tattoos that I knew about. "What does Winter have to do with it?" I asked.

"Well, whenever Winter does something, you suddenly want to do it, too," Mom said. Which was a complete falsehood, because I had no desire to set foot in Sarah Borne.

"I was just wondering," I told her. But I remembered

the notebook and my observations. This would be the perfect time to show Mom. I started by asking, "Why is Winter still going to Sarah Borne? Can't she go back to public school?"

"She absolutely could, if I would let her," Mom said. "And though I shouldn't have to explain my decisions to my ten-year-old daughter, I will tell you that I want to make absolutely sure that Winter remembers her time at Sarah Borne. It will prevent future mishaps."

Future mishaps had already been prevented, I thought, since Winter was keeping all her stories extra-secret. I told Mom that maybe her plan was working too well, pointing out how depressed Winter was all the time and pulling out my notebook for her to read.

Mom read through the entire list of observations without a single "Hmm," or "Oh no," or even "Heavenly Donuts!" After a few minutes she handed the notebook back to me and said, "Star, I know teenagers. When I was pregnant with Winter and I thought my life was over, I was very depressed. But it was just a phase. Now Winter's going through similar feelings, even if she is being a bit overdramatic about it. When you're a teenager, you'll find out. Even the smallest, most insignificant things can make you feel like the whole world's out to get you."

Maybe Mom was right. And if she was, maybe I was overreacting, thinking that my failure of a club was a hopeless mess that couldn't be saved.

I mean, it *is* a good club.

It just needs more people.

Star Mackie

September 25

Week 2 Vocabulary Sentences

NEW AND IMPROVED!

1. Once during the summer Mom and Winter got into a huge argument about school and California and gas money. Winter threw a lamp that shattered against the wall and fell to pieces, and then two seconds later Gloria came in the door with a big pink box of donuts, and she said, "Who wants donuts?" all singsong and happy, and the silence after she said that was awkward.
2. When we lived in Brookings, Oregon, we boycotted a lot of things. Mostly department stores, unless there was a clearance sale, but I remember once Mom boycotted the electric company because she didn't have enough money to pay the bill. That was actually fun, because we got to use candles for a few months.
3. A lot of the trailers at Treasure Trailers are derelict. Winter says it's because people who live in trailers already know they've hit rock bottom. Mom says it's

because trailers are hard to maintain. Gloria says the rust spots give her trailer personality.

4. There are at least five different people in Treasure Trailers who fit the description of gaunt, but Gloria says they are just drugged-out. So I guess that girl's mom was right? Unless "drugged-out" is different from "drug-addicted."
5. No one uses the word katzenjammer, Mr. Savage, but I will try: everyone in Treasure Trailers—at least Mrs. O'Grady, though she says she knows a couple others who agree—is in a katzenjammer about the broken-down vending machine in front of the owner's office that keeps eating one-dollar bills without giving anything back.
6. Some of the perils of living in a trailer park: sometimes cars crash into your trailer, and sometimes the cops come by and ask a lot of questions even though they're actually looking for the guy in the next lot who already moved out.
7. The dump is across the fence from us. If I were a criminal escaping from the police, I would hide there, behind the enormous trash piles. And then I'd be taking refuge in refuse. Get it?
8. My mom had her very own scandal. When she was nineteen, she had my sister, Winter, and she wasn't

married. Gloria said it was a big deal, even in the nineties.

9. Every day I traverse my way to school, since Mom says, "It's only twelve blocks" and "Ask me again how far I used to walk to school, Star, go ahead."
10. I only have one memory of my dad, and it's sort of vague. We were at the county fair, and I was on the Ferris wheel, so I only saw him from far away. The thing I remember most clearly about that day is that after I got off the Gravitron, I threw up.

CHAPTER 11

I didn't turn in my sentences again this week.

Why? Because when I handed them to Winter Thursday morning so she could look them over before she left, she read through them and handed them back, saying, "Do you want Social Services knocking on our door?"

No. I didn't. Nobody wanted Social Services knocking on their door. Social Services hated people who lived in trailer parks. It's like they have it on a checklist of things parents can't do if they want their children living with them.

Winter patted my shoulder and said, "You know teachers are mandated reporters, right?"

Yes, I knew. Teachers were always talking to Social Services about kids who had bad parents or filthy houses. Winter and I didn't have either, but teachers and social workers didn't always see it that way.

"Okay, now you want to know what I see in your sentences, if I'm pretending I'm a mandated reporter or some Social Services jerk?"

She told me what my sentences really sounded like:

Sentence 1: Lots of fights happen in the Mackie household, and things get thrown and broken.

Sentence 2: Ms. Mackie can't pay bills.

Sentence 3: The Mackies live in a derelict trailer park.

Sentence 4: The Mackies live among a bunch of junkies.

Sentence 6: The Mackies just really don't live in a very good place, do they?

Sentence 7: The Mackie children think it's okay to play in a dump.

Sentence 8: Ms. Mackie was a single teen mother.

Sentence 9: Ms. Mackie makes her ten-year-old child walk to school by herself.

Sentence 10: The thought of her father makes Star Mackie think about throwing up.

Which meant that sentence 5 was the only good one, but probably only because Winter didn't even know what a *katzenjammer* was. (I told her my theory that Mr. Savage throws in one weird word every week.) I thanked Winter and traversed my way to school, trying to at least stay in crosswalks instead of jaywalking like I usually do, so that if a Social Services person did come by, it wouldn't look so terrible.

As soon as I got to class, I headed for the trash can to throw my sentences away. And on my way back to my desk I swear someone stuck a foot out, because I tripped where I don't usually trip. Everyone scowled at me, too, even Mr. Savage. Especially after I told him that I didn't have any sentences for him.

He was probably mad that I hadn't even brought last week's sentences, like he'd told me to. I'd spent a lot of last night going over my Winter notebook. Then, after doing one set of sentences, I hadn't really felt like redoing the old set. Especially since I already knew all the words and how to use them in sentences.

I kind of hoped he'd just walk away again, like last time. Maybe tell me to bring them next week. But, instead, what he said was, "They're really not that hard, Star. You should be able to get them done." I hated the way everyone's stares felt after that, like I was too stupid to manage something as simple as sentences. Didn't it even occur to Mr. Savage that I had done them, and I just happened to leave them at home for the second week in a row? Why did he have to suddenly assume that I was a delinquent?

Especially since I've turned in everything except the stupid vocabulary sentences.

I thought about retrieving and keeping the sentences as proof that I'd actually done them, but by the time recess came around, I just didn't see the point, so I left them in the trash.

Where they belonged.

CHAPTER 12

As soon as Mom left on Saturday for her job interview, Winter jumped out of bed—fully dressed—and said, "C'mon, Star, let's hit the mall." She was in such a good mood, I thought maybe Mom had been right. Maybe this was just a phase. (I still think Winter should get to go back to public school, though.)

I pulled on tights, a jean skirt, and my worn-out pair of combat boots. They used to be Winter's, back when she was thirteen. She used to lace them with rainbow shoelaces and paint splotches of nail polish on the toes to make them look blood-splattered. The nail polish has chipped off, but they're comfortable and warm and keep the rain out.

That's what I say to Mom when she asks me why I wear them every day instead of the almost-new high-tops she bought me. The truth is, I don't like my high-tops because they make my feet look flat, like duck feet. But Gloria says Mom spent a lot of money on them, thinking that I'd like them, since they were just like the ones she used to wear. I didn't want to be mean, so I told Mom I'd wear them when it stopped raining. Which I hoped was never.

Today was a good day to be wearing combat boots, because the puddles from last night's rain hadn't dried up, and the clouds right above Treasure Trailers looked like they were about to explode. We jumped into the pickup, and after Winter started the engine, I noticed the gas needle hanging right above *E*. I remembered Mom saying a couple of days before that Winter's gas would have to last her through the weekend, but Winter didn't seem worried. We practically flew out of Treasure Trailers, and in the rearview mirror I thought I saw the tinfoil man's tinfoil-covered blinds moving.

Then Winter said, out of nowhere, "Don't you think it's a little weird that we're not allowed to talk to Dad?"

"I thought it was the other way around," I said.

"Yeah, me, too," Winter said. "But I've been thinking. I mean, he sent me that card. Maybe he was hoping I'd, like, find him."

Just you? I thought, trying to remember the line he'd written at the end. *Hope you and your sister are doing well.* It didn't seem like much, but it was proof that Dad hadn't completely forgotten about me, like I'd always assumed.

Because even though Mom wouldn't let him talk to us, even though she said that she refused to let him walk in and out of our lives whenever he wanted, it was obvious that he did care. About Winter, at least. Mom and Gloria had never said anything, but I kind of already knew that Winter was Dad's favorite. She'd gotten the truck, after all, and the card, and she was the one he'd wanted to see at the fair, not me.

Mom had tried to convince me that I'd wanted to go on the Ferris wheel so much that I didn't care about seeing him, but that wasn't true. I remember trying to lift up the metal safety bar and crawl out of my seat, even though I was thirty feet up in the air. When I think about how close I was to seeing him, my ribs still ache.

But when I think about that line, *Hope you and your sister are doing well,* it's like I'm back on the Ferris wheel again, except it's coming back down this time, and Dad's waiting there on the ground for me.

"Do you want to come with me?" Winter asked.

I whirled my head around to face her. "To the mall?" I asked. We were practically there already. The big marquee in the parking lot blinked out a 40 percent off sale, but I didn't catch where before it switched to the time and temperature.

"No, silly. To see Dad. Were you even listening?"

"We're going to see Dad?" I didn't care about the mall anymore. I wanted Winter to make the most illegal U-turn possible and drive us to Dad right then. "You know where he lives?"

Winter said he'd put his address on the card envelope and that she'd memorized the street name and number. "We know he still lives in Brookings," she added. Gloria had let that slip a long time ago.

But that was a problem. Dad lived in Brookings, and while we used to live just outside of Brookings, we were now living about a hundred miles south of the Oregon border. On the worst highway of all time, 101. It wouldn't be so bad if it didn't run along so many cliffs, or if it had more than one lane once in a while. It made for long, headachy trips.

I glanced again at the truck's fuel gauge, where the needle was still hovering over the *E*. We'd probably need a full tank of gas to get to Dad and back.

Winter agreed. She said we probably wouldn't be going for a while, since she needed to secure some funds. I didn't know what that meant, so Winter explained that

Mom would know something was wrong if Winter blew an entire week's worth of gas in one day.

That's why we were going to the mall, it turned out. We weren't buying anything. Winter just needed a job. I offered to contribute the five dollars I had in my coin purse back home, but Winter told me not to worry about it as she pulled into a space outside the food court.

According to Winter, the food court is a revolving door of teenage workers. We started there and walked through the entire mall, one store at a time, Winter asking for job applications and me holding the ones she'd already gotten. I could picture Winter working in pretty much any store—except Style Cuts, of course. We made sure to avoid that one and the ones next to it, even though Gloria wasn't working that day. After all, Gloria's always going on and on about the other stylists and who thinks who's too fat and who thinks who's too skinny and who thinks whose styling credentials are fake. Clearly, they are all gossips.

It took us an hour and a half to get through all the stores, and then we sat down in the bookstore café so Winter could fill out the applications. That took another two hours. I looked for a book about clubs and didn't find any, not even in the Dummies section. I doubted Dad would be impressed when I told him my club had only two other people in it.

Maybe I was worrying too much, though. I'd only had one meeting, and clubs always start out small before getting bigger. Someone would probably join next week. Genny might have some friends who could come, and then I could finally make some friends, even if they were fourth-graders.

Satisfied, I left the self-help section and instead went and read the backs of all the Stephen King books. (He's a writer like Winter, but his stories are less bloody.)

When Winter finished, we went back through the mall, dropping off the applications. Most people said, "We'll call you," while shoving the application into a drawer under the cash register. A few people looked over what Winter had written and asked, "Can you come by tomorrow for an interview?" By the time we left the mall, it was raining. Anyone who says California is nice and sunny has never set foot in the state.

Not that I cared that much, because before long we'd be back in Oregon anyway.

CHAPTER 13

I stayed up late on Tuesday preparing for the club meeting. Mom kept telling me to go to bed, but she was staying up late, too, trying on different pairs of pants and skirts and blouses and earrings. She had another interview, to be a receptionist at a radio station. Every five minutes she'd turn to me and ask if something made her look too old. Then she'd say, "Don't answer that. You should be asleep."

I filled five whole pages of my club notebook with questions and conversation topics and trivia. Some of it wasn't even trailer-park related, but I was hoping that no one would notice.

And I was right!

No one noticed, because Genny and Denny were the only two people who showed up.

Genny got ready to take the minutes, and I considered pulling out my notebook for about half a second before Denny's glare switched from his desk to my face.

That's when I just gave up and plunked my head down on my desk.

"What about a different club?" Genny suggested, while my head was still down. The cool wood was kind of refreshing. "I mean, we both like trailer parks," she said, and I didn't have to look up to know that Denny was rolling his eyes, "but it'll be hard to talk about them for a whole year."

"That's a good point," I told the desk. "Put that in the minutes."

Genny's pencil scratched against her paper, shaking the desks a bit.

"A drawing club could be good," she said. "I know some girls who like to draw. Denny, do you know anyone who likes drawing?" Denny didn't reply, or else I didn't hear him. "Or how about a writing club?"

"We can't do a writing club," I said. "My sister started a creative writing club at her old school, and it got her into trouble. Now she has to go to Sarah Borne." Denny made a weird sound, like a snort-grunt, so I picked my head up off the desk and asked him what was so funny.

"Nothing," he said, and actually looked like he meant it.

"Our brother goes to Sarah Borne, too," Genny told me. "He got picked on at his old school. It was so bad, he'd cut class all the time, so he failed everything."

"Half brother," Denny said, like that didn't make them real brothers at all. "And he got picked on because he wore makeup."

"It was eyeliner," Genny said. "Oh, and nail polish. And he has a lip ring."

I couldn't picture this so-called brother. I kept seeing an older Denny, but an older Denny would never wear makeup or nail polish or any kind of ring. "Can we take a field trip to your house?" I asked. "I have to see this to believe it."

Genny pumped her fists like this was a great idea, but Denny stood up so fast his chair flew backward, making Mr. Savage glance up from his stack of papers.

"You're not allowed to come to our house," he said, grabbing Genny's arm, "and neither is your sister!" He stomped out of the room, dragging Genny, who looked as confused as I felt. After the door closed behind them, Mr. Savage raised his eyebrows at me for an explanation.

"Um. He had to go. Suddenly."

"Okay, then." He went back to his papers, humming,

scratching his beard with his pen, and I went to pick up Denny's chair.

Honestly, I didn't care that Denny hated me so much, since the feeling was pretty mutual. But how could he hate Winter?

He'd never even met her.

Star Mackie

October 2

Week 3 Vocabulary Sentences

1. These sentences are complicating my life a bit, so I'm going to sit here on my bed and just find stuff in my trailer to write about.
2. Mr. Savage, your weird, old-fashioned words that haven't been used for a hundred years make me want to defenestrate my dictionary. Why is that even a word, when you can just say, "I'm going to throw my dictionary out the window"?
3. If I stretch out of my bed a bit, I can see to the back of the trailer, where Mom has hung a glimmering crystal in the window. The same window I may end up throwing my dictionary out of.
4. Our trailer is immobile, because it never moves, despite having wheels. For some reason this trailer has only two wheels, which are in the middle, so we have to prop our home up with cinder blocks to keep it from becoming a seesaw.
5. I don't know if I would call anything in our trailer lavish except for maybe the collection of fancy soaps

in the bathroom. Mom won them in a raffle, and no one is allowed to use them. They just sit on the bathroom sink looking pretty.

6. I presume that if I used the fancy soaps, my hands would smell good and feel like a bed of fresh-picked rose petals. I would also be grounded.
7. Therefore I would regret using the fancy soaps, since the grounding would last longer than the good-smelling hands.
8. I promise this will be the last sentence about fancy soaps, but it's your fault for choosing the words: I would ruefully promise my mother that I would never again use the fancy soaps.
9. There's a picture on the fridge that Mom calls Gloria vs. the Ultimate Donut. It was the ultimate donut because it weighed three pounds and also because it was the only donut Gloria could never finish.
10. My sister and I share a wardrobe, kind of. I get all her old clothes, but mine wouldn't fit her. Have you ever read the book The Lion, the Witch and the Wardrobe? I haven't, but why are a lion and a witch sharing clothes? How does that work?

CHAPTER 14

I really wanted to turn in my sentences this week. They turned out pretty good, and I made extra sure they did not include things about junkies and dads and bills.

I had them out, ready to hand to Mr. Savage as he passed my desk. But before he got to me, he was in front of Meg Anderson—the fourth-grader who was always cleaning out her desk and who always had her homework ready—and she told him that she'd left hers at home.

"Meg, I'm disappointed," he said, which didn't sound bad, but judging by how red Meg's ears turned, she didn't like hearing it one bit.

"Yeah—well—but—" Meg said, her ears turning redder

with each word. Then she pointed to me and yelled, "Star didn't turn hers in either!"

I gasped, and it was the only sound in the room. Mr. Savage turned his beard in my direction, and I knew from the way he clenched his jaw that I was in trouble. Before I even had time to point at Meg and remind him that she was the one who left her stupid sentences at home, Mr. Savage stomped his way over to my row.

"This is not acceptable," he said. We all shrank down in our seats. I don't think we'd ever seen Mr. Savage mad before. "Don't think I don't know what's going on. Maybe the vocabulary words don't seem that important. Maybe because I've been letting certain people get away with not turning them in, week after week."

I hated how he'd said that, *get away with,* like I was some kind of juvenile delinquent. And I hated that everyone in the room knew who he was talking about, because they all turned in their seats to look at me.

"So, everyone else who doesn't have sentences today, raise your hands," Mr. Savage said.

At first, no one did. Maybe it was out of fear. I thought, for a second, that it was just Meg Anderson who'd forgotten, and that she'd actually forgotten, because even smart people forget things sometimes. Like the one time Winter left her pepper spray in her locker, and the next day happened to be the day the principal searched it.

I was still planning on handing Mr. Savage my sentences, with one of those smiles that says, *See? I'm totally not a delinquent like you think I am, even though I haven't redone the last two weeks yet,* and then—

To my left, a hand went up. And to my right, a hand went up. And somewhere in the back corner, another hand went up. Three whole hands. Maybe Mr. Savage was right and they really had decided not to turn in their sentences because of me. Because I was *getting away with* it.

I felt this hard poke right in my back, and Delilah hissed at me, "Star! Raise your dang hand!" And Denny was turned all the way around and glaring with full force, and even stupid Jared was telling me to put my hand up. Mr. Savage's eyes stayed on me, and he made this "up" sign with his hand so that he was saying it, too, and everywhere I looked, someone else was saying the same thing.

Everyone really thought I was some kind of juvenile delinquent.

So I put my hand up, because I was tired of having to prove that I wasn't. I wondered if this was how Winter had felt last year, after her third and final trip to the principal's office. Did she know that no matter how much she tried, no one would ever look at her the same way again?

But that wasn't true. There was one person who didn't think Winter was a delinquent, besides me, because he hadn't seen her in years and hadn't even said anything to her since she was thirteen.

That must be why Winter wants to see Dad so much. *Hope you and your sister are doing well.* It doesn't seem like much, but he hopes. Maybe because he knows things will get better.

When the bell rang for lunch, I dropped my sentences into the trash, and hoped.

CHAPTER 15

Fifth-graders have detention on Fridays in Miss Fergusson's room, which is next to Mr. Savage's room on one side and the school garden on the other. Miss Fergusson's room has a couch with a quilt that you can tell was handmade. There are names stitched into it, and before she told me to sit my butt down, Miss Fergusson said each name was done by one of her former students.

I wish I'd gotten Miss Fergusson for fifth grade. Her hair bounces when she walks, and she has kind, brown eyes that match her skin perfectly. Plus, when some big-eared jerk asked why my hair was so stupid, she told him that if he didn't have something nice to say, he could write it on the whiteboard in perfect cursive one hundred times.

But no, instead I'm stuck with Mr. Savage, who sent only me to detention and let all the other kids who didn't do their sentences finish them at recess. At recess, he made me wash desks. And then after class he said that *obviously* I couldn't hold any club meetings in his room until I had turned in all my sentences.

But that was kind of a relief. Now, instead of having to say that my club was so bad that no one wanted to join it, I could tell everyone that, actually, Mr. Savage had just canceled the whole thing before anyone could join.

I bet Miss Fergusson wouldn't have canceled my club. And I bet she never would have told me it was a terrible idea for a club, even though it was.

I ended up sitting in a back corner, far away from the other delinquents, who all looked like they lived in detention. There was one kid sitting next to me, though, and I couldn't figure out why he was in there. For the whole hour he did nothing but sit at his desk and read a book. And not a normal book, either, but one of those thousand-page paperback books that are starting to yellow with age, the ones that always pop up at porch sales. This one didn't have a cover, though. Someone had ripped it clean off.

I wanted to see what he looked like, but the boy had his book so close to his face that all I could make out was his hair exploding out of the top, dark brown and curlier than Winter's. His hair was just a little bit darker than his hands, and he seemed a little taller and a little wider than all the other fifth-graders. When detention ended, I thought I'd see his face finally, but he left with it still buried in the book.

Outside, all the other detention junkies from the fourth and sixth grades stood around in their little groups, talking. Book Boy was out on the lawn talking to some sixth-grader with a mohawk. They were talking about the coverless book, I could tell, because Book Boy kept pointing to it, and Mohawk Boy kept throwing his hands up in the air. I got close enough to hear Mohawk Boy say, "I think it was him," and then I had to jump out of the way, because Book Boy came barreling right past me and up to a group of sixth-graders.

The group stopped talking, and he held up his book and said, "This look familiar to anyone?"

The whole group took a big step backward, except for one boy, whose whole face had stretched into shock. "Eddie, I didn't know it was yours," he said, and before he could say another word, Eddie slammed his fist into the side of the boy's head.

I gasped. I couldn't help it. Eddie swiveled on the spot and squinted at me, like he couldn't believe anyone would have the nerve to be even remotely surprised at the sudden punching. Then his mohawked friend came and grabbed his arm, and he forgot all about me.

By the time I got to the trailer, I still hadn't figured out which was worse: doing three weeks of sentences for the world's worst teacher or spending another Friday in detention with a boy who probably wanted to punch me, too.

CHAPTER 16

Apparently Winter got a job on Tuesday and didn't tell me, but Saturday was her very first day of work. I wanted to go with her to the mall, and I promised I'd stay out of the way and only come by once an hour, but Winter said she had to face this one on her own. She did promise to bring me home a soft-baked pretzel with hot mustard, though.

I stayed home with Mom and Gloria, since it was Gloria's day off. Mostly she complained that it was raining and she couldn't go to the duck pond and that the stale cake donut she'd been saving was totally going to go to waste.

"Get your microwave fixed yet?" Mom asked.

"Heavenly Donuts, I think I need a priest to exorcize it," Gloria said. "I want to find out if someone died in that trailer before I got here. Tinfoil Man's not talking, but I know there's something weird going on with my lot. Eat a donut, Star." She handed me a maple round from the box on her lap. I looked to Mom to see if that was okay, since it was almost lunchtime and we usually don't eat dessert first. But Mom just kept talking to Gloria, so I bit into my donut and got cream filling all over my shirt.

"How's school going, Star?" Gloria asked as I dug through the utensil drawer for a napkin.

Mom answered for me. "She's doing real good. I think California's a good fit on her."

I guess no one had told her about my having detention, but I certainly wasn't going to be the one to break it to her. "It's hard to make friends," I told her instead. "They're all a bunch of house-dwellers." I wished there was a harsher word for people who didn't live in trailer parks, something as bad as *trashy*, but the truth was, no one made fun of you for living in a house.

"You don't have any friends yet?" This was from Gloria.

"Well, I kind of have one friend, but—" I started, before Mom cut me off.

"When I was growing up, all I had was Gloria," she said. "Sometimes I got teased, especially once when I got my hair cut too short. It made me look like a boy. But Gloria just gave 'em the elbow, and that was that."

"Yup. Your mom did the same for me."

They gave each other a best-friends hug, even though they're both over thirty, and I guess I should have informed them that Genny was not exactly my best friend or my friend, period. She was probably the closest thing to a friend that I had, but since her only competition was Denny, it wasn't that hard. It's not like we were having sleepovers and putting false eyelashes on each other. Genny had offered me one of her tattoos the other day, but that wasn't quite the same.

Besides, I couldn't imagine Genny giving anyone the elbow.

But when I tuned back in to Mom and Gloria, ready to ask for advice and pointers and an elbow demonstration, they were in the middle of a conversation.

"Maybe a cat died in there or something. You know old Mrs. O'Grady's always going on about her missing cats."

"Yeah, sure, Carly. I'm being haunted by a cat."

They'd gone right back to the microwave.

CHAPTER 17

I knew Monday was going to be terrible, because someone put banana peels in my desk, and then the hot lunch was a gray-colored beef stroganoff that smelled like a basket of dirty laundry. I was starting to think Winter had the right idea about being a vegetarian.

Just like every day, I chose a seat at the lunch table with the fewest people at it. Then I had a silent stare-down with the stroganoff, and it won. I shoveled a couple of noodles into my mouth before I noticed Denny and Genny heading over.

They set their sack lunches down across from me and sat down. I have no idea why Denny was there, but Genny said right away that we needed to talk about the club.

"What club?" I asked, because I was pretty sure the Trailer Park Club had been disbanded by Mr. Jerky McBeardface.

"Our new club," she said. "We just need a new angle and a new teacher, and then we're back in business."

"Back in the business of being the only three people in a club?" I asked.

"That's what the new angle's for," Genny told me as she peeled all the salami slices off her sandwich and piled them in front of Denny. "We'll get more people in this time."

I couldn't help smiling, even though Genny didn't know what she was talking about. Maybe she can't elbow people like Gloria, but she doesn't give up—that's for sure. So I said, "I'll think about it."

Denny choked on his salami after I said that, so I figured that might be a sign that Monday wasn't going to be so bad after all.

CHAPTER 18

When we got back from lunch, Mr. Savage had a poem written on the chalkboard. I probably wouldn't have cared so much about it, except:

Hope is the thing with feathers
That perches in the soul,
And sings the tune without the words,
And never stops at all,

And sweetest in the gale is heard ;
And sore must be the storm
That could abash the little bird
That kept so many warm.

I've heard it in the chillest land,
And on the strangest sea ;
Yet, never, in extremity,
It asked a crumb of me.

—Emily Dickinson
December 10, 1830–May 15, 1886

Whoever she was, Emily Dickinson had the exact same birthday as Winter! (Except the year.) The poem was good, too, and when Mr. Savage started talking about Emily Dickinson Week and our new vocabulary words, I just tuned him out so I could reread it over and over again.

The thing I liked about it was that it was about hope, so it was kind of happy, but there was something sad in there, too, like Emily Dickinson had written it on a very bad day. She must have been like Winter, then, writing to make herself happy. I wondered what other poems she'd written and whether the library had any books about her, and did she know that *soul* and *all* didn't rhyme very well?

Maybe she knew and she just didn't care. I could picture a critic telling her that the poem didn't rhyme right, and her saying, "Rhyme this!" and punching the critic in the throat.

When the bell rang and everyone rushed out the door, I raced over to Genny's desk and said, "Let's start a club about Emily Dickinson."

CHAPTER 19

There was no way I was having my new club in Mr. Savage's room. Even if I'd been allowed, I wouldn't have wanted to anyway. I wanted Miss Fergusson's couch and quilt, and when Genny asked if we could hold the club in her room, she said yes! We just had to do it on Monday afternoons instead, which was fine.

It had to be Genny who asked, just in case Mr. Savage came poking his beard around and asking questions. He'd only said I couldn't have the club *in his room*, but I knew he'd be like Mom and say, "You know what I meant!" if he found out.

But Miss Fergusson thought it was a great idea for a

club, and she lent me a book full of Emily Dickinson poems to read, with the poet's stern face plastered on the cover. "And," she said, fixing her brown eyes on mine, "I have a student who I think would like to join this club."

Which was perfect, just perfect, because I knew I wouldn't be able to invite anyone from my class without Mr. Savage finding out. So I thanked Miss Fergusson and shook her hand, all the while pretending not to notice the glare Denny was shooting me from over by the door.

For the next few days, I paid extra attention whenever Mr. Savage talked about Emily Dickinson and wrote down everything he said in my old Trailer Park Club notebook. Every day he put up a different poem, and every day I copied it down.

On Wednesday, our creative writing assignment was to write our own Emily Dickinson–inspired poem. I wrote:

In the Winter!
We get Snow –
But – in the Trailer!
We Don't Know –
Where Autumn Ends!
And Winter Starts –
'Cause Winter's There!
Inside our Hearts!

Most of the poems Mr. Savage had put up were just like that, with dashes everywhere and random words capitalized for no reason. Mr. Savage didn't tell us why Emily Dickinson did that, but I'm guessing it was her way of cheering herself up. When you see her face, you can tell it hasn't smiled very often.

We had to exchange poems with someone else, so Jared read mine and I read his. This part wasn't so great. Jared was really confused by my poem. He said, "So you don't have a calendar?" and "Are your hearts all frozen?"

So I had to explain that it wasn't about winter the season, it was about Winter the sister. Which made Denny groan in his seat, but I'll take that over glaring any day.

Jared told me my poem sucked, but he had just copied one of Emily Dickinson's poems and changed a few words, so his poem started just like hers: *I'm Jared! Who are you? Are you Jared, too?*

I'm so glad he's not going to be in the club.

Star Mackie

October 9

Week 4 Vocabulary Sentences—Emily Dickinson

1. Emily Dickinson is excused for using the word abstemiousness because she was actually alive when people last used it. But fine: Gloria doesn't have any abstemiousness when it comes to a large box of donuts, and she'll eat the entire thing. (So why she couldn't eat a three-pound donut is beyond me.)
2. There are a lot of very obvious comparisons between my sister and Emily Dickinson, which is why I think I like her poems so much.
3. You can tell that Emily Dickinson was an eccentric person from all the random dashes in her poems, but if you only looked at her picture, you'd think she just sat in a rocking chair all her life, picking petals off flowers or something.
4. There doesn't seem to be any extremity to Genny's tattoos. She just plants fresh ones over the ones that have already flaked off. Is there a bucket in her room that's just full of tattoos?

5. I was supposed to be idle about my sentences this week, but all of our words are from Emily Dickinson poems, so I actually want to know what they mean.
6. Lately Winter is very listless about her hair—or, more specifically, her roots. So I've become listless, too, because dyeing roots is something Winter and I always did together.
7. Plummetless wasn't in my dictionary, which means Emily Dickinson made up words. Or maybe her dictionary plummeted into the ocean, which would also explain why she capitalizes things that shouldn't be capitalized.
8. I've been recollecting an old memory of my dad. It used to be vague, but now that I've been thinking about it every night, it's gotten clearer. Some nights I even sneak outside onto the steps of the trailer, because the cold breeze reminds me of being at the top of that Ferris wheel.
9. Emily Dickinson dropped out of college, and Winter was expelled, so you could say they were both spurned by their schools.
10. Everything Emily Dickinson wrote was kind of in vain, because she died before people even read her poems. I hope that doesn't happen to Winter. I hope one day people will read her stories without expelling her.

CHAPTER 20

I'm starting a sentence boycott. This time didn't count, because I needed to know the words for the club, and besides, I just threw them in the trash as usual. I had to stop myself from giggling several times when Mr. Savage was standing next to the trash can, because it was so funny that they were right under his beard and he didn't even know it. Genny thought it was funny, too, when I told her at lunchtime.

Then she asked why I was throwing my sentences away.

So I told her, "I'm boycotting sentences. I've been doing them the whole time. I've just never turned them in."

Denny coughed and said he was going to get some milk, grabbing Genny's quarters on his way. Genny asked if she could join the boycott, but I don't want her getting detention, so I told her I had it covered. But it was nice of her to offer, I thought, considering no one else had. They'd all turned in their sentences this week, and now that Mr. Savage was giving me detention every time I didn't turn mine in, I didn't think anyone was going to try and get out of doing them again.

Since Genny couldn't boycott sentences, she decided to boycott her organic chocolate pudding and gave it to me, and when Denny came back and saw me spooning the pudding into my mouth, he scowled.

"You're supposed to eat that," he told Genny.

"It's basically milk, which I already have." And she took one of the milk cartons Denny had brought back. "Mom won't care."

Denny glared at me like it was all my fault. I tried telling him Genny had given it to me, but my mouth was full of organic chocolate pudding. Which I don't think tastes that much different from regular chocolate pudding anyway.

After school Genny and I went to see Miss Fergusson again so we could hang a flyer up in her room. I asked if she had anyone else in mind for the club besides the student she'd mentioned, and she said, "Yes, I also know a sixth-grader who's planning on joining. He's even named after a famous poet."

"There's a boy named Emily?" I asked.

"Different poet," Miss Fergusson told me.

Denny was waiting outside, and for once he didn't yank Genny's arm and drag her away from me. Instead, he walked behind us with his hands jammed in his pockets while Genny and I worked out all our club details.

"That's five members so far that we know about," Genny said. "We're gonna need a sign-in sheet. We could elect a treasurer!"

"Do treasurers do anything?" I asked.

"I don't think so."

"Okay, that can be Denny's job."

By the time we got to the front entrance, we had next Monday planned out. Surprisingly, Genny is full of good ideas. Just as I was about to ask her if she was still going to take the minutes, she gasped, pointed to the street, and said, "Denny, look! It's Winter!"

And it was. Winter's pickup was parked at the curb, with Winter inside. The giant pair of sunglasses sat on top of her head, keeping strands of curls out of her eyes. When she saw me, she waved, stepped out of the truck, and straightened out her skirt. Her high heels clicked against the pavement as she jogged over to me.

"Hey, Star. I figured I'd pick you up today."

"I thought you got out after me," I said, but I only

thought that because I never actually saw Winter until way after coming home from school.

"We had early dismissal," she told me. Then she looked a little to my right, and her eyebrows jumped up her forehead. "Oh. Hi, Genny."

Genny's mouth, Gloria would have said, was like a manhole without a cover, and her gaze darted between Winter and me and back again. "You know her?" she said, I think to both of us.

"We're sisters!" I told Genny, and then I realized what *she'd* said. "*You* know her?"

Genny turned and yelled, "Denny! Did you know that Star and Winter are sisters?"

Denny glared down at his own shoes.

"Mom wants to know when you're coming over again," Genny said to Winter, and this time I had the manhole mouth. "And Allie won't say. Saturday would be best, 'cause we're having quiche. And it won't have any meat in it."

With one quick motion, Winter pulled the sunglasses over her eyes. "Um. We'll see."

"Okay. Denny! Come *on*!" Genny turned and ran over to her brother, grabbing his arm and dragging him down the block. Which was weird, but not as weird as both of them knowing who Winter was. I heard Genny's voice even as she got farther away. "Let's go tell Allie! He's probably home now! They got early dismissal!"

After they were out of earshot, Winter said, "You didn't tell me you knew the Libras. Well, come on, let's go."

Winter let me get into the truck first so I wouldn't have to walk in the street. Then, after she got in and had started the engine and was moving along with traffic, I said, "How do *you* know them?"

Emily Dickinson could have written a poem about the sigh Winter gave me, including words like *regret, sadness,* and *willow tree*. (Emily Dickinson always puts in plants or animals.) When she finally finished her sigh, she said, "I kind of went out with their brother Allie. Over the summer."

I reviewed all the things I knew about Genny and Denny's brother: he went to Sarah Borne, he wore eyeliner, and he had a lip ring. Denny doesn't seem to like him. Oh, and he's their half brother, not their full brother. "What does he look like?" I asked. "Is he cute?" Denny looked like a long, skinny rat.

"Uh, kind of," Winter said. "Like, in a pathetic way. We broke up a while back, but I guess he hasn't told his family yet. They always freaked me out. Like, they're a little too happy, you know?"

I thought of Genny and nodded, but then I thought of

Denny and said, "I don't think Denny knows how to be happy."

"Is he the one with the staring problem?" Winter lifted up her sunglasses and did such a perfect impression of Denny's glare that we both burst out laughing, and the truck swerved a little too close to the sidewalk. Luckily we were on the street near Treasure Trailers, so there weren't any other cars around. Winter pulled up to the entrance and said, "I'm not driving on that gravel, so I'll let you out here."

"Okay." I'd forgotten that Winter was just giving me a ride home. I guess I assumed she'd come back to the trailer with me. Maybe because I had so much to tell her about the Emily Dickinson Club, and my sentence boycott, and detention, and, and, and. "Where are you going?"

"Work," she said. "Those pretzels won't make themselves." Leaning across the cab, she kissed me on the side of the forehead and added, "We get paid Friday, but I won't have enough for our Dad visit for another two weeks. Plus, I gotta find a place that'll cash checks and not charge too much."

I gave her two thumbs up and jimmied open the creaky door so I could jump out. Maybe I should have been disappointed that we wouldn't be seeing Dad until the end of the month, but it was nice to have a little more time. By *this* Friday, all I'd have is two week's worth of detention.

But by the end of the month, I'd have myself an actual club and actual friends.

And Dad would want to hear all about it.

CHAPTER 21

Detention was the same as last week, with less punching. Even though I sat on the opposite side of the room this time, I was still positive that Eddie would be over at any second, fists flying like a couple of windmills.

But Eddie just sat there reading his book. He was the quietest kid in detention, but no one would sit by him. Probably because of the punching.

My new seat was awful, and I regretted moving, because now I was closer than ever to the other detention junkies. They all side-eyed me, and then side-mouthed to one another, probably about me, while Miss Fergusson was engrossed in her grading. I guess it wasn't that bad—

all I had to do was make sure I was the last to leave and pretend not to hear the girl who said my hair was the color of toilet cleaner. None of these delinquents know midnight blue when they see it.

Outside, the front entrance was as busy as ever. Eddie sat on the steps, completely absorbed in his thousand-page book, so I thought I'd be able to sneak by without being noticed or squinted at. But that was a big bust, because his mohawked friend was sitting right next to him, asking Eddie over and over again what he was reading. When Eddie didn't answer, he asked if it was a kissing book. And when Eddie still didn't answer, he made kissing sounds until Eddie shoved him off the steps. He stayed sprawled out on the ground like that was exactly where he wanted to be, and my covert escape plan was ruined, because I had to step right over him to leave.

"Hey," he said to me. "Nice mullet."

Layered cut, I thought but didn't say, because even though I was sure Eddie wouldn't hit me without a reason, I wasn't so sure about his friend.

CHAPTER 22

I spent the whole weekend at the library, except for the times when the library was closed. I spent those hours either in Gloria's car or in Gloria's trailer or in our trailer. Not a whole lot of time in Gloria's trailer, because every time I open the door and the microwave turns on by itself, my heart jerks.

In the library, I must have skimmed every book about Emily Dickinson they had. I knew a lot about her already, from my vocabulary sentences and the books Miss Fergusson had lent me. But I still learned a few cool things, like how she had a sister (a sister!) and how she'd had her heart smashed to bits when some guy wouldn't marry her.

Everything I read just proved that Emily Dickinson and

Winter were almost the same person. Winter's heart may not be smashed, but I can tell she's carrying a big sadness inside her. The other night, after Mom had fallen asleep, Winter told me she hasn't been turning in all of her homework. "I thought I'd be able to do it at work," she said, "but people are always wanting pretzels." I pointed out to her that Emily Dickinson had dropped out of school completely, and she was still a great writer.

"Yeah," Winter said, but the word was heavy with sadness. I hoped that seeing Dad would make that sadness go away.

On Monday, as soon as the last bell rang, Genny and I raced to Miss Fergusson's room, while Denny lagged behind. We said hi to Miss Fergusson, and she told us to go ahead and push some desks together. The couch looked so comfortable, but I guess only three or four people would be able to sit on it at one time, not an entire club. So Genny pushed five desks together, and then I squeezed a few more desks between them in case even more people showed up.

And then we waited.

Denny shuffled in, found a desk, crossed his arms, turned his glare on, and sat.

We waited some more.

Genny tapped her pencil against the paper she had out

to record the minutes. The clock was being slow on purpose, I think, and I ended up arranging and rearranging and straightening all my papers a hundred times. Just as I was about to ask Miss Fergusson where her so-called promised club members had gone off to, the door to her room squeaked open, and two pairs of feet scraped against the floor.

It was Eddie and, behind him, his mohawked buddy. Heading right for our cluster of desks, pointing at me and saying, "Poetry Club?"

I glanced behind me, to make sure he wasn't talking to someone else. "Um, Emily Dickinson Club," I told him.

"Yup," he said, instead of "Whoops" or "Oh, sorry, wrong room." He tossed his backpack onto the nearest chair, where it thudded, as if the bottom was lined with cement.

"Good job being on time, boys," Miss Fergusson said.

"Thanks!" said the boy with the mohawk. "And I would like to say, Fergie, that you look radiant today."

"Flattery didn't get you far last year, Langston. Just take a seat."

"You got it!" And Langston, the boy with the mohawk, sat right next to me, as if there were no other available chairs anywhere in the room. "Hey, I know you," he said, fixing his sunken eyes on me. "You're Mullet Girl."

Before I even had time to think *layered cut,* Genny was

leaning over her desk with her arms out, like she wanted to choke someone. "Her name is Star Mackie, not Mullet Girl, okay? And you have the stupidest hair here, so you can just shut up!"

I think if Mr. Savage had popped in at that moment to tell us all that I was his number one student, I couldn't have been any more surprised.

"Genny!" Denny said, whirling on his sister, and she settled back into her seat, eyes blazing. I could tell then that the glare ran in the family but that Genny only used it for good, unlike her brother. Unfortunately, it had no effect on Langston, who put his feet up on the desk and leaned back in his chair.

"He doesn't know when he's being insulted," Eddie said to the group, and then, as if he were in charge or something, added, "So what're we gonna read first? How about 'Because I could not stop for Death'?"

"We have to take minutes first," Genny said, as if *she* was in charge.

"We are going to introduce ourselves," I announced, slapping my hand on the desk so hard it stung. "That is what we are going to do. And we're all signing in." I grabbed one of the papers off Genny's desk and wrote my name on it in huge letters. "I'm Star," I said, handing the paper to Langston.

"We should also say one thing about ourselves," Genny said, which was a good idea. Why hadn't I thought of that?

"Okay. I'm Star, and . . ." I couldn't think of what to say. It was obvious that I liked Emily Dickinson, and telling people I lived in a trailer park had not gone very well before. So I said the next thing that popped into my mind: "I'm going to see my dad in a couple of weeks. My sister and I. We're both going." I paused. "It's going to be a lot of fun."

"Cool," Langston said, still writing. "I'm Langston. I probably won't see my dad again until June. We always spend the summer together."

"Eddie," said Eddie. "My dad's black."

We all stared at him.

"I thought we were talking about dads or something," he said, shrugging.

Genny waved and introduced herself. "My dad builds chicken coops and stuff," she said. "We see him every day."

Denny was last. His glare had faded away. He said, "I'm Denny." We waited. "Genny and I have the same dad."

"Okay!" I announced, maybe a bit too loudly, but only because we'd already wasted two whole minutes and we had a mountain of poems to read and categorize. Every one of Emily Dickinson's poems fit in one of three categories: nature, God, or death. The plan was to vote on which ones belonged where. "We're going to start

with"—I flipped through the papers for a poem that was *not* "Because I could not stop for Death"—"Aha! Here we go. 'A bird came down the walk.'" I took a deep breath to start the poem.

"'He did not know I saw,'" Eddie said. "'He bit an angle-worm in halves and ate the fellow, raw.'"

My breath stalled in my throat. He was saying the same words that were on my paper. He was saying the poem *from memory*. "Wait a second," I said, halfway through the second stanza. "How did you . . . ?" I didn't know what to ask, exactly. "Did you go to the library?"

Eddie laughed, kind of like a dog barking one sharp, loud bark. "We're not allowed at the library since *some-body*"—and he stared very pointedly at Langston—"got caught drawing bras on the covers of all the magazines."

"I'm not ashamed," Langston said. "And if Emily Dickins-worth were alive today, I think she'd be okay with it. I'm very good at drawing bras."

"Say the word *bras* one more time, and I'm kicking you all out of my classroom," said Miss Fergusson, without looking up from her papers. Genny wasn't even taking minutes, I noticed—she'd locked her hands over her mouth to keep from laughing.

And Denny was glaring at me like this was all my fault.

"Okay, we're not talking about—" I almost said it. "*B-r-*

a-s. We have poems to read. *Read*, as in *read* from a paper!" Taking the papers in one hand, I rustled them at everyone in turn. When I got to Eddie, I asked, "How did you know that poem?"

"I know a lot of poems," he said.

Winter once had to memorize a poem in junior high, and I remembered that she'd practiced for hours in front of the mirror before she had it down. "Are you really smart or something?" I asked, which set Langston off. He nearly tumbled off his chair laughing.

"Smart!" he said. "He got held back in first grade 'cause he didn't know how to read!"

I expected Eddie to start punching, but he just crossed his arms, frowning. "Yeah, I didn't know how to read until I got Mrs. Flower in second grade. She made me stay after school so she could teach me how to read with a bunch of poems and crap. Easy rhyming ones, not the hard ones. She had this big book full of poems in her desk, with gold-rimmed pages and everything, and she said I could have it if I could read one of the poems inside without any help."

He unzipped his backpack then and took out a thick red hardcover book. The pages gleamed gold, and so did the title, *America's Best-Loved Poems*. "When we're done with Emily Dickinson, we can use this," he said.

"What do you mean, *when we're done with Emily Dickin-*

son?" I asked. "This is the Emily Dickinson Club. We're never going to be done with Emily Dickinson!"

But no one was listening, and Genny was already reaching out for Eddie's book, and next to me, Langston had somehow gotten ahold of the paper with all our names on it, and at the bottom he was drawing a girl in a bra.

The whole time, Denny kept glaring at me, except his mouth had twisted into an evil little smile. He knew as well as I did that the first meeting of the Emily Dickinson Club had gone horribly, horribly wrong.

I was going to need a word ten thousand times stronger than *vexation*.

CHAPTER 23

I popped into Miss Fergusson's room during lunch recess for the next few days to ask if anyone else—anyone at all—had asked about joining the Emily Dickinson Club. She told me there had been "no further interest as of late." She also said that Eddie was a nice boy and to give him a chance, but then I saw him at recess shoving Jared into the tetherball pole and cussing out one of the playground monitors while Langston stood nearby laughing, and I thought, *Nope.*

"Did you ever have anyone in your writing club who you didn't want to join?" I asked Winter Wednesday afternoon while we shared a plate of carrots and ranch dressing. Normally she wouldn't have been home, but she'd been sick with the stomach flu for the last few days. She wasn't supposed to be eating anything either, since everything she ate made her throw up, but she was feeling better today and was going to risk it.

"No," she told me. "I just didn't let people in if I didn't like them, so it worked out pretty well. Or not, you know, since I still got expelled. You mind if I put some mustard in this?"

I shrugged, wondering if I was anywhere close to expulsion. "They can't expel you for not doing homework, right?" Winter said they couldn't, and I relaxed a little. I told her about Eddie and Langston, who were probably way closer to being expelled than I was. I'm positive the reason no one else will join the club now is because of them. They were scaring people away. "And now they're taking over my club and making it about bras and . . . and other poems . . . and they act like they're the ones in charge . . ."

"So be in charge," Winter said, picking up a big glob of mustard with her carrot. "It's your club."

She was right. It was my club. I'm the one who started it, and I'm the one who needed it. But how was I supposed to take charge of it?

I think if I'd known that this club would be so much work, I wouldn't have started it in the first place. But of course now that I'd gone through all the trouble of keeping it alive behind Mr. Savage's back, there's no way I'd ever give it up.

Not even to Eddie.

(Unless he tried to punch me.)

Star Mackie

October 16

Week 5 Vocabulary Sentences

I'M NOT TURNING THESE IN!!

HA-HA-HA-HA-HA!!!!

1. I will commence turning in sentences when Mr. Savage shaves his beard. (This is not going to happen, because he loves that beard and scratches it at least three times a day.)
2. Until then I am confined to the classroom during recess, where Mr. Savage makes me wash desks. I don't think they can get any cleaner at this point, but he doesn't seem to care.
3. Washing desks is the opposite of exhilarating, so while I'm wiping my rag back and forth, I think about other things so it doesn't seem so boring.
4. Meanwhile, Mr. Savage sits at his desk, which has probably not been washed in a million years, considering the mound of papers and the dying plant on it.
5. Because I am perpetually dipping my hands in and out of a bucket of water, it has chipped off all my

midnight blue nail polish. I'd repaint my nails, but they'd just chip again in no time.

6. I have a whole phantasmagoria of things I'd rather be doing running through my head while I wash desks, like throwing my bucket of dirty water on Denny and taking all of Mr. Savage's weird, old words and throwing them into a volcano.
7. I also think about the day when everyone in class stops ridiculing me. It hasn't come yet, but I think it's close. I mean, no one's called me Star Trashy for, like, two days, and that's a record.
8. I also think about how I can get more people to join the club. I don't even need everyone to join it, I realized—just a significant number of people. Enough to make everyone else want to join.
9. For that to happen, I need to be absolutely swaggering, the way Eddie is. I even practiced in the mirror a little bit, but Gloria just asked me why I was acting so scared of my own reflection.
10. For now I just have to tolerate Eddie and Langston being there, at least until someone else joins or I figure out how to keep them away.

CHAPTER 24

I sat in my usual spot in detention, near but not next to the rest of the detention junkies, on the opposite side of the room from Eddie. But Eddie, who did not have his thousand-page paperback book in front of his face today, got up from his usual desk and sat next to me.

Which made all the other detention junkies pick up their things and move to the other side of the room.

They *were* afraid of him!

"Hey, listen," Eddie said to me, and Miss Fergusson was cutting us some slack, I think, because detention was about to start and Eddie wasn't even trying to whisper. "Miss Fergusson said I should apologize for interrupting you and being loud and all that other crap at your Poetry Club."

"Emily Dickinson Club," I said.

"Whatever." He pulled the red hardcover out of his backpack and put it on my desk. "Here, you should borrow this. It's got a bunch of different poems in it, and they're all really good."

I opened the book to the table of contents and said, "Does this have any Emily Dickinson poems in it?"

"You're really obsessed with her," he said, shaking his head.

I started to tell him how she reminded me of Winter, but Miss Fergusson apparently decided she was done with the slack and shushed us from her desk. Detention had begun.

Eddie dug his big coverless book out of his pocket and started reading, and because I had nothing better to do—and *only* because I had nothing better to do—I flipped through *America's Best-Loved Poems*. The book was obviously bogus, because it only had one Emily Dickinson poem, "Hope is the thing with feathers." Which I already knew by heart but reread anyway.

It's a weird poem, because it didn't fit into any of the three Emily Dickinson categories. It's not about God or death, and it seems like it might be a nature poem because it has a bird in it, but it's not actually about a bird, it's about hope. Hope is just a thing with feathers, so it could be anything. Anything with feathers.

I also wondered why Emily Dickinson thought about hope that way. When I thought about hope, I didn't think about anything feathery. Recently, I'd started thinking about my dad whenever I thought about hope. Maybe because I was hoping to see him soon, or maybe because of the line he'd written on Winter's card.

Before we came to California, I'd never really thought about Dad much at all, and now here he was, in my head, making me hope for things like birthday cards and ice cream dates and whatever else fathers and daughters did together.

Sometimes when I can't sleep at night, I'll half dream that I'm back on that Ferris wheel. I'll see Dad from way up high, and I'll reach my arms out. I'll want to touch him, and I can't, and when I open my eyes, I'm still in the trailer.

I think there's been this empty space in my heart where Dad was supposed to be, and I'd never noticed it before, since Mom won't talk about him and neither will Gloria.

But now that Winter and I are going to see him, it kind of feels like the Ferris wheel is moving again, bringing me closer and closer to Dad. Close enough to jump out and see whether he has brown eyes like mine, or gray ones like Winter's.

I took out my notebook and opened it to a fresh page to write, *Hope is a Ferris wheel*. It was supposed to be the start of another Emily Dickinson–style poem, like my Winter poem, but after a few minutes of tapping my eraser on the desk, I gave up trying to think of what the next line was and just wrote, *It spins and spins and spins*.

I glanced over at Eddie, wondering what he thought hope was, or if there was something he was hoping for. But probably not.

I almost ripped out my poem, but even though it was only two lines, and not a very good poem, I figured maybe someday I'd be able to finish it.

CHAPTER 25

I lugged Eddie's stupid red book all the way home, because when I tried to give it back, he asked me what poem I'd read, and when I told him I'd read "Hope is the thing with feathers," he got this disgusted look on his face and told me to keep reading.

Why is he even in the Emily Dickinson Club if he doesn't like Emily Dickinson?

We had a full house when I got back to the trailer: Winter sitting up in bed, looking pale and a little sweaty and insisting she felt fine; Mom in the bathroom, digging through the box of medicine, talking about doctor appointments; and Gloria at the counter, smelling a box of donuts but not yet eating them.

I grabbed a sprinkled cake donut from Gloria's box and sat down at the table. "Why does Winter have to go to the doctor?" I asked Mom.

"Because she's had the flu for nearly a week," Mom said, at the same time Winter said, "I *don't* have to go to a doctor! Everyone's overreacting!"

"It'll be a quick trip, Winter," Mom tried, but Winter shook her head back and forth violently. "I've got to take you to the doctor. I'm responsible for your welfare."

"You're responsible for *putting* us on welfare," Winter told her.

Mom didn't shrink an inch. "I guess I walked into that one," she said. "Now, where'd I put our insurance cards . . . ?"

"Probably in the shed, Carly," Gloria said. Mom had a box labeled IMPORTANT STUFF that she kept in our storage shed, and it was a huge mess that contained everything from old pay stubs to medical records. For the first time I wondered if there was information about Dad somewhere in there. Mom kept the key in her room, but I didn't know where.

"Look," Winter said. "The only reason I threw up was because I ate some meat yesterday."

"Heavenly Donuts!" Gloria said. "What kind?"

"Pepperoni pizza."

"So does that mean you're done being vegetarian?"

Mom asked, with a hopeful lilt in her voice. I hoped so, too, because while I wanted to be vegetarian with Winter, I really liked meat. There was no way I could give up ground beef and fish sticks and fried chicken.

But Winter wasn't done, she said. Since eating meat had made her throw up, she wasn't touching it again for a long time. Mom wilted a bit, but she didn't shrink, and Gloria held up a maple-bacon donut and said, "I guess I'm eating this one."

While Mom and Gloria went out to the grocery store to get Winter some ginger ale, I took Eddie's book out of my backpack and flipped through some of the pages.

"What's that?" Winter asked.

I told her about the book, about how Eddie wanted me to read poems that weren't by Emily Dickinson. "Maybe we shouldn't have just Emily Dickinson poems," I said.

Winter jumped off the top bunk, her feet thudding against the floor and shaking the trailer a bit. "Is this that kid who was trying to take over your club? I thought you were going to take charge of it again!"

"I want to," I said, closing the book. "I just don't know how." At this rate, I'd never get anybody else to join the club. I took out my club notebook to look at my notes and all the pages of Emily Dickinson poems I'd copied.

Winter sat down across from me at the table and said,

"You're not just reading them poems, are you? Everyone will get bored if you do that."

"Um." I kept flipping pages, trying to find one that didn't have a poem on it. There was Emily Dickinson's life story, which I'd copied out of the encyclopedia at the library . . . which was also probably going to bore everyone. I was about to give up when I landed on my not-even-half-finished poem, "Hope is a Ferris wheel."

"Maybe we could all write our own poems," I said, mostly to myself, but then I remembered that my own poem was not even half-finished, and if the club president couldn't finish writing a poem, that wasn't a good sign.

"Hope is *what*?" Winter said, trying to read my writing upside down.

"A Ferris wheel."

"Oh. That sounds good," she told me. "But I don't really get it."

Me neither, I almost said. Instead, I reread the poem to myself, thinking that hope could be a lot of things.

And then I had it.

I yelped, making Winter flinch, and shut my notebook, shoving it into my backpack. Eddie's book went under my bed, where I hoped it would stay for a long, long time. Because if my idea worked, there was no way we'd ever be done with Emily Dickinson.

CHAPTER 26

Genny and I only put out five desks today for the Emily Dickinson Club, because the way I figured it, if anyone else came to join, that meant they weren't afraid of Eddie or Langston, and they could drag their own desks over.

While Genny wrote the names of all in attendance, I thumped my fist on the desk like a gavel. "Emily Dickinson said 'Hope is the thing with feathers,'" I started. "I thought maybe we could come up with our own ideas about what hope is." It didn't quite sound as in charge as I wanted it to, so I thumped my fist again on the desk. "I think it's a Ferris wheel," I said.

"Why a Ferris wheel?" Eddie asked.

"Because it spins," I said.

Genny scribbled something into the minutes.

"And?" Eddie said. "What does that mean?"

Which was terrible, because I hadn't thought that far ahead. I'd need some time to figure out how to explain it. "You all have to write yours down first," I said. "And then I'll tell you."

Everyone except Denny asked for paper and pencils, which Miss Fergusson got out of her supply closet for us. She asked, "May I join in, too?"

"Sure!" I said, and she took a piece of paper back to her desk.

After about five minutes I asked if everyone was done, but no one except Langston was. After five more minutes Genny was done. After five *more* minutes, Denny and Miss Fergusson finished. And last, three minutes later, was Eddie.

I decided we should go in reverse order, so Eddie went first.

"Okay, this might sound dumb," he said, and the look in his eyes said that if we thought it sounded dumb, he had a fist he'd like to introduce us to, "but I think hope is a rock. Because you can squeeze it all you want, and you can't destroy it. *But*." He leaned in close, eyes wide. "It can still be crushed." Then he slapped his hand on the desk, and we all jumped back.

"Oooooooh," Genny said.

"Don't put any of that in the minutes," Eddie told her, and Genny started erasing fast.

Miss Fergusson was next. "Hope is September," she told us from her desk. "That's when I get my new students. I always have so much hope for them." She mostly said this to the back of Eddie's head.

Denny said hope was dust in the wind. I was actually impressed, because I'd expected Denny to not even try. But then Genny said he'd gotten that line from a song, and Denny went back to glaring at his lap.

Genny read hers: "Hope is everywhere. It's a meadow full of bees. They go buzzing by."

"Mine doesn't seem that dumb now," Eddie said.

"It's a haiku!" she said. "Okay, what did Langston write?"

Langston held up his paper to reveal a drawing of Emily Dickinson wearing a bra.

"Okay, well, unless Langston does it, too, I'm not explaining mine," I said, staring him down.

Crumpling up his paper, Langston told us that hope was a dirty window. "You can't see through it all the way. You just figure there's something good out there."

"Langston," Eddie said, pretending to choke up, "that brought tears to my eyes." Which made Langston throw his crumpled-up bra drawing right at Eddie's face. Eddie started to get up, and I banged my fist again, and suddenly everyone's attention was on me.

I was nervous, because everyone else's ideas about hope were a lot better than mine. But Eddie said, "Come on," and Langston said, "You promised," and Genny said, reading back over the minutes, "She didn't promise, but she did say she'd tell us."

"Just don't laugh," I said. So I started by telling them about the day at the fair, my only memory of Dad. I was six, and Winter was twelve, I knew for certain. And it must have been the first time we'd ever gone to the fair, because Mom always tells us that fairs and carnivals are money traps. Other than that, some details I had to make up, while others kind of popped into my head as I went on.

I guess I was the only one who wanted to ride the Ferris wheel. Mom and Winter promised to wait for me, so I took my ticket and stood in line, next to a woman whom Mom asked to ride with me so I wouldn't be by myself. By the time we got into the basket, Mom and Winter had gone, and before I could tell the woman to let me off, the basket lurched forward and up so fast, my stomach flipped.

The higher I got, the more of the fair I could see, and

soon I spotted Mom's straight black hair next to Winter's blond curls (it was before Winter started dyeing her hair). They were standing by the hot dog stand with a man I'd never seen before. From far away he was blurry, like Mom and Winter were, but I could tell a few things about him: he was tall (like Winter) with a red baseball cap (neither of us likes baseball) and a black leather jacket (we both like black).

When the Ferris wheel reached its highest point, I saw the man put his hand on Winter's shoulder, and that's when I started to yell. The bar holding us in was locked tight, though, and there was no hope of me getting out. The woman sitting with me must have thought I was just scared, because she put her arm around me and told me to close my eyes.

But I didn't. As the Ferris wheel came down again, I watched him walk away. Soon he was out of sight. And the next time my basket reached the top, he was gone, gone, gone, and Mom and Winter were back where they'd said they'd be.

The first thing I said to Mom when I got off was, "Who was that man?"

She hesitated for a second. Maybe she thought I hadn't seen him. "Your father."

"Where did he go?" I asked.

"He had to leave. I'm sorry, Star, but I knew you really wanted to ride the Ferris wheel."

The Ferris wheel! Of course I'd wanted to ride the Ferris wheel—I was six! But I wanted to see my dad more. Mom should have known. I could have ridden the Ferris wheel anytime, but that was my one chance to meet Dad. It's weird: I didn't feel so bad about it while we were at the fair, aside from throwing up on the Gravitron, but as soon as we got ready to go home, I began to cry.

Winter tried to make me feel better by saying that he hadn't said much anyway. And that he was old and smelled kind of like rubber.

It did make me feel a little better. And when we got to the car, I leaned down to smell one of the tires so I'd know what he might smell like. Besides, the way Mom had always talked about him, it never seemed like he cared about me at all, so I tried hard to not care about him either.

But since then he'd hoped I was doing well. And I hoped that he would be happy to see me.

"So," I said, at the end of my story, "hope is a Ferris wheel, because you can be far away from something, really wanting it, and the wheel can bring you closer. And sometimes you can step right off, but sometimes the wheel doesn't stop spinning, and you keep moving around and around in a circle. But you never lose sight of what you want." Even though I had lost sight of Dad that day, I thought that was pretty fitting.

Everyone nodded after I finished. I looked over at Langston, and he had another piece of paper. Guess what he was drawing.

We read a few more Emily Dickinson poems, which Langston said all sounded the same. Eddie smirked at me, and I knew he was smirking about his stupid *America's Best-Loved Poems*. But I smirked right back, because I'd taken charge of my club.

And now I could convince other people to join.

Star Mackie

October 23

Week 6 Vocabulary Sentences

STILL NOT TURNING THESE IN!

NOT NOW, NOT EVER!

1. I have accumulated a lot of sentences so far. By the time I get to the end of these, I will have accumulated sixty sentences! (Even more! Because usually I write more than one sentence for each word, despite the instructions.)
2. I am deliberately not turning them in, but they're still fun to do. The best part will always be throwing them away, though.
3. Which is a little sad, considering all the time I'm forfeiting just to do them. All the time it takes to look up the words and make sure they're alphabetical and think of the best way to put them in a sentence—I could be doing a million other, better things.
4. Like planning my club. Next week's meeting is looming, and I still don't know what I'm going to do to keep everyone interested and stop them from interrupting

just because they think they know more than I do.

5. And by everyone, I mean the four other people in the club, the club that was supposed to be a lot more prosperous than it turned out to be.
6. And I just spent ten minutes looking up the word quagga, and it's a zebra. Wait! It's an extinct zebra. When am I ever going to use—okay, fine. I rode a quagga to school in South Africa two hundred years ago when that was still possible.
7. All that time spent looking up quagga could have been spent packing for our trip on Saturday. We're going all the way to Oregon, and we're finally going to see Dad. What I've packed is scant. I'd like to bring all sorts of things, but we can't fit much in the truck. So what should I bring to show him?
8. I can't bring trinkets. I should bring something really important instead. Something that will let Dad know what I'm like. I have to pick out an outfit, too. Something clean without any holes.
9. So it is nice to do these sentences, to be able to write everything out and keep myself off the verge of panicking.
10. But I'm still not turning these in, even after spending all this time on them, because that is my wont, and I don't think it will ever change.

CHAPTER 27

It took me forever to get my Dad bag packed, and I ended up packing hardly anything. Just a couple of homework papers and projects I got stars on, and my Emily Dickinson poem—the one Jared said sucked. I'm pretty sure Dad will like it better.

I spent Friday's detention making a list of things I wanted to talk to Dad about, like my club (hopefully he'll have some good advice), and how Mr. Savage is a terrible teacher, and what Mom was like when she was younger. Maybe he can tell me how they met, because Mom won't tell me anything except that they went to community college together.

Other than that, detention was pretty dull, and even if

I wanted to talk to Eddie, he was working on some math paper the whole time. Miss Fergusson gave him a big smile when he turned it in at the end of detention, but I'm not sure he noticed. He caught up with me in the hallway and asked if I'd read any other poems yet.

"I've been busy," I told him.

"Oh, okay," Eddie said, and I thought that's what he really meant and that he'd drop the whole poem thing, but a couple of steps later he started to recite this poem from memory. It was short and kind of funny, but it didn't make any sense. He said it was by someone named Gwendolyn Brooks and asked me what I thought.

"I think Emily Dickinson wrote two thousand poems," I said. "I think if we do one poem a week, we'll be set for life."

We were almost to the front steps, when Eddie put a hand on my shoulder and shoved me a little bit. Not enough to knock me over, just enough to steer me into the edge of the hallway.

"What was that for?" I asked.

"For being so stubborn," he said. "Is that why you're in detention? I've been wondering, 'cause it's not like you're a bad kid or anything."

I said it was none of his business why I was in detention, and he muttered, "Yup, I knew it."

We sat down on the steps, and Eddie started another poem. This one was by Robert Frost, and it was almost as good as one of Emily Dickinson's poems, but when I told Eddie that, he said, "I hate Robert Frost."

"Then why did you even recite it?"

"Because I knew you'd like it, since you have the worst taste in poetry," he said, and I felt like shoving *him* just a little bit, enough to knock him down a step.

Langston appeared then, plopping down right next to me and saying, "Hey, Mullet." I wondered if he even remembered my name.

While Eddie recited some more poems, Langston used a wood chip to chisel the dried mud out of the lugs of his boots. At one point he asked me how long my fingernails were and if I would mind trying to dig into this one little crack in his sole, because he was pretty sure there was a rock there, and he'd do it himself except he had a bad habit of eating his fingernails. Eating his fingernails. *Eating his fingernails.*

I used my pencil instead. Langston asked if eating fingernails was one of those things that boys did that girls did not like, and I looked him right in his sunken eyes and said, "*Yes.*"

When I finally got home, I couldn't believe it was 5:30. But the microwave said it, and so did the clock on the wall, and so did the answering machine when I checked the messages. I even asked Mom and Gloria, who were sitting at the built-in table talking about some girls they'd gone to high school with, and they both said the same thing.

I just couldn't believe I'd spent a whole hour sitting on the steps with Eddie and Langston, talking.

Why couldn't they be people I actually wanted to be friends with?

CHAPTER 28

While Mom made dinner, something noodle-y with bell peppers and carrots, I checked on my Dad bag, which I'd hidden under my bed. It felt like something was missing. What else was I supposed to bring? Since Mom had never taken us on a Dad trip, I had no idea. I tossed in my club notebook, in case Dad had any ideas for it, and, at the last second, Eddie's big red poetry book. I was determined to find a poem, a good poem, so that he would have to take back what he'd said about my taste in poetry.

"Do you have a favorite poem?" I asked Mom as she dumped a Gloria-sized portion onto my plate.

She chewed on the end of her wooden spoon for a

moment, then she said, "'Two roads diverged in a yellow wood . . .'"

"No, no," I told her. "That won't work."

"What about 'The Raven'?" Gloria said. "'Said the raven, Gimme more!' Isn't that how it goes?"

"That doesn't sound like a good poem," I said, and then I told them both to forget about it, but of course they didn't, and they just came up with one bad poem after another, their laughter shaking the table. Luckily Winter came home a few minutes later.

"Ah, Winter graces us with her presence," Gloria said.

"Don't you have an appointment to go ruin somebody's hair?" Winter said back to her. Then, letting her backpack fall to the floor, she turned to Mom. "I was thinking maybe I could take Star to the redwoods park tomorrow."

"Redwoods," Mom scoffed. "You know we had redwoods in Oregon? California acts like they own all the redwoods in the world." We'd never visited the redwoods when we lived in Oregon, but I think sometimes Mom likes ragging on California the way the rest of us do.

"So can we go?" Winter asked.

"I don't know why you're asking me," Mom said, dropping her fork on the table. "Usually you just do whatever you want, and I find out about it later." Which was unfair, because if Winter was doing whatever she wanted, she'd be sneaking off to the public high school every day.

Still, I hoped Winter would not start a fight with Mom. An angry Mom would not let us go anywhere tomorrow, and we'd be stuck inside with nothing but Gloria's rented copy of *Beverly Hills, 90210: The Third Season*.

Winter swallowed, took a breath, and said, "Well, I apologize. May we please go to the redwoods tomorrow?"

Mom stuffed a forkful of noodles into her mouth and chewed slowly. We all watched her throat bob as she swallowed. "Fine."

I smiled at Winter, and she smiled right back before heading straight for the fridge. "I made this vegetarian, you know," Mom told her, but Winter said she really wanted a grilled cheese sandwich and asked if there were any pickles. We only had the sweet kind that Winter and I hate, but she ate some anyway.

Once I was done eating, and after Mom went to walk Gloria back to her trailer, I checked my Dad bag one last time. "Is there anything else I should bring?" I asked Winter. I wanted to bring him our whole trailer. I wanted him to see all the things he'd missed for the last ten years.

"It's not like we're gonna stay overnight," Winter told me. "Just bring yourself. That's what I'm doing."

So I zipped up my bag and put it in the truck and worked on my outfit. I had a couple of clean skirts but figured the black one would be best so I could match Winter. And I grabbed the one shirt I owned that Mom had bought at a department store clearance sale instead of at St. Vincent's, along with my least-frayed pair of tights.

But my combat boots were a problem. They were so old and scuffed. I reached under my bed for the high-tops Mom had bought for me. They really did look almost new. I put them on, just to try out, and, yup, they still made my feet look flat. Maybe Dad was like me and would like the combat boots better. Even if they weren't as new.

I put the boots with the rest of my outfit and chucked the high-tops back under my bed, making sure Mom wasn't watching. And then there was nothing left to do but wait for tomorrow to hurry up and get here.

It was a lot like being on the Ferris wheel again and finally coming down to the ground. It was the slowest part of the ride, but at least this time I knew that when I finally got off, Dad would be there waiting for me.

CHAPTER 29

Mom microwaved us some breakfast burritos. She was still in her robe, which was odd, because she always likes to shower first thing in the morning. Then Gloria came over with a small bag of donuts and her big bag of hair-care products.

"Gloria's gonna touch up my lowlights," Mom said. "Then we thought we'd hit a couple of thrift stores. What time will you girls be home?"

Winter said maybe around dinner, and Mom said, "There's that many redwoods to see?" and Winter said, "It takes a while to drive there, you know." Then Mom gave Winter a few dollars for lunch, and we headed out the door.

"Hey, Winter," Gloria said as she set her bags on the table. "When are we going to deal with those roots of yours?"

"I think I'm just gonna let the dye fade out," Winter said. Already Winter's hair had faded into a rusty sort of reddish-black, but it was permanent dye, so it still had a couple of months before it finally croaked. So that was doubly surprising, especially since Winter hated having blond hair. It made her look too nice, she always said. No one was going to buy bloodbath horror novels from a girl with blond curls.

As we got into the pickup, I thought about letting my dye fade out, too, but once the blue faded, I'd be left with a bunch of white streaks in my hair. I'd look like some kind of mutant skunk. Langston would call me Skunk Girl.

Mrs. O'Grady came out of her trailer while we were buckling our seat belts. We could barely make out her head over the portable fencing. "Tell your mother to stop stealing my newspapers!" she yelled, and then her hand appeared, shaking a broom at us.

Winter yelled back, "Okay, Mrs. O'Grady!" And then muttered to me, "Who steals some old lady's newspapers?"

We drove out of Treasure Trailers. I guess since it was now less than a week until Halloween, everyone was decorating. Some people replaced their Christmas lights with orange and black Halloween lights. Even the guy in the tinfoil-covered trailer had a tinfoil-covered jack-o'-lantern sitting in front of his steps.

"Are you really not going to dye your hair again?" I asked. "I thought you liked black." I know *I* liked Winter better with black hair, because it made us look more like sisters.

"I just want it to grow out a bit," she said. "I'll dye it again eventually. I just . . . don't know when."

"When you go back to public school?" I asked.

"*If* I go back to public school."

Of course she'd go back to public school. I told her that, but she didn't reply, and her lips pursed tightly together like she didn't want to say anything at all.

Maybe she was as nervous as I was. But I wanted to talk, talk, talk. I wanted Winter to tell me about the time she'd talked to Dad at the fair, or any other time she'd seen Dad. Hadn't she seen him when she was really little, before I was born?

Instead, I opened the glove box and let all her stories fall into my lap. Winter reached over, plucked one from the pile, and held it out to me. The paper was bright and new, the folds crisp. A brand-new story! Maybe the first that Winter had written since school started in September.

"What's this one rated?" I asked.

"Probably R," Winter told me. "But only for violence. And some language."

The story was about a girl who's at a party with a boy she likes, at a house by a dark and dreary lake. The boy dares her to drink some of the lake water, which is icy cold going down her throat. The next day she feels sick, but her mom won't let her stay home. She goes to school and feels sicker and sicker and sicker, and it feels like her insides are being sliced apart. But no one believes her when she says how much pain she's in. Finally, at the very end of the story, she goes to the bathroom, thinking she's about to throw up. But instead, a giant gross maggot bursts out of her stomach.

That's how it ended.

"So, she's dead?" I asked. "And then, does the maggot get bigger and bigger and start eating all the girls who come into the bathroom?"

Winter laughed and said, "Hey, that's pretty good! Maybe you should write some stories."

"I wrote a poem," I said, thinking about my Emily Dickinson poem. The first one, about Winter, was tucked safely in my Dad bag. "No one liked it, though."

Winter told me no one had liked her first story, either, back in elementary school. She'd written about some radioactive gum that made the girl chewing it melt into her desk. "You'll get better," she said.

I didn't think so, considering my unfinished second poem. But that reminded me of the poetry book I'd brought along, so I asked Winter if she wanted to hear some poems, and she said sure. We were out of town now, and the traffic had thinned out, though the highway still had two lanes instead of one. Trees rose up all around us. Redwoods, which meant we could tell Mom we'd actually seen them.

I flipped through Eddie's book, looking for short poems, and read them to Winter, and we voted on whether they were good or bad. Most were somewhere in between, which I planned to tell Eddie to prove that Emily Dickinson really was the best poet in the world.

"See if 'The Tyger' is in there. It's by William Blake," Winter told me. "I bet you'd like it."

I flipped to the table of contents to see, and found, at the very bottom, that someone had added a title in pencil. Sloppy pencil, like a really little kid had written it. It said, *Amarica's Gratist Poem*, followed by lots of dots and the number 548. So I flipped to the very end of the book, past the index, and into the blank pages that are always at the back of a book.

There, written in the same sloppy pencil, was the poem

"The Bagpipe Who Didn't Say No" by Shel Silverstein. I must have said the title out loud, because Winter said, "What?"

I knew this poem. Everybody in the United States probably knew it. It's about a turtle who falls in love with a bagpipe, but the turtle gets his heart broken, because bagpipes don't have feelings.

"This is not a great poem," I said. I couldn't believe Eddie had written it in there, but who else would have done it? No one, because then they would have been punched across the playground, even if they were a little kid. "He doesn't know anything about poetry," I told Winter, snapping the book shut.

"You got your club under control?"

"Yeah, I think." The book went back into my bag, but now I wished I'd just left it at home. "I still have to come up with something for next week, but I don't want to. Or maybe Dad will have an idea." That would be good.

"Yeah," said Winter. "I hope so, too."

That word, *hope*, stood out, and I asked Winter, "What do you think hope is? Eddie said it was a rock."

"You talk about Eddie a lot," Winter pointed out. "Hey, look. The ocean."

I'd seen the ocean before, and besides, with all those darkish clouds in the sky, the ocean looked gray and swampy. "I thought it was a good answer," I told her. I could hardly remember what everyone else had said about hope. I mean, Genny's was a haiku, and it didn't even make sense.

"Well, maybe he does know something about poetry," Winter said. I told her he got held back in first grade, and he used to be a bad reader, and now he went around punching and shoving people, sometimes for no reason at all.

"I think he's the reason no one else will join the club." Also Langston—Langston wasn't helping. "Plus, Eddie wants to stop doing Emily Dickinson. He wants to do all the other poems in the world. Anyway, what do you think hope is? You didn't answer yet."

Winter smiled and said, "I know." And then, just as little sprinkles of rain began pecking at the windshield, she said, "Maybe a raindrop. It goes hurtling to the ground, aiming for a puddle or a lake or the ocean, so it can be with all the other droplets."

I'd known that Winter would have a good answer, but I hadn't expected it to give me chills. It was like she was describing me, except I was hurtling through school and hoping to make some real friends.

I looked around for a pen to write it down—on my arm, if I had to. But then Winter said, "Usually, though, it just splatters against the cement. Sometimes hope isn't enough, Star. Remember that."

I told her I would, but for the rest of the ride I stared out the window and tried to forget.

CHAPTER 30

His name was plain old Robert, and his house was bigger than three trailers combined. Tall green shrubs guarded his lawn instead of a fence, and his paved driveway, with two brand-new trucks parked in it, was miles away from any dump. The only bad thing I could say about the house was that it wouldn't stop raining outside. It always rains in Oregon.

Without our umbrellas or raincoats, the walk to the front door was much wetter than I would have liked. Winter's curls sagged with the rain, while my hair clung to the back of my neck.

We rang the doorbell but didn't hear it go off inside. I hoped he would be the one to answer the door, not his wife, because, according to Gloria, his wife didn't like Mom at all, and so she probably wouldn't like us either.

Luckily he did answer, pulling open the door and looking from Winter down to me and back up again, like he couldn't understand what two soaked girls were doing standing on his porch. His gaze lingered on Winter for a few extra moments before he said her name. "Winter?"

She nodded, and if the smile on her face was a clue, she was too happy to speak. Instead, she wrapped her arms around him, and after a second of surprise, he did the same, hugging her tightly. "It's been years," I heard him say into her shoulder, and then he looked at me and said, "And this must be Star."

My heart swelled. If Emily Dickinson had any poems about hearts, I bet she would have described them as balloons. "Hi," I said, and my bag felt suddenly heavy. There was so much to tell him, to show him. How was I going to get it all out?

"Come inside," he said, inviting us in. His house was so warm, warm enough to walk around barefoot. Which I presumed he did most of the time, judging by the basket of shoes by the door. And he didn't smell like rubber at all, I noted as soon as he turned to close the door. He smelled like . . . fresh laundry.

"Does Carly know you're here?" he asked, and then he

answered his own question. "Of course not. She'd throw a fit. Come on, both of you. Take off your shoes. Let's go sit by the fire."

Heavenly Donuts! He had a house with a fireplace!

I couldn't wait to go back to school on Monday and tell the next person who made fun of my trailer that my dad lived in a big house with a fireplace and that his carpets were spotless.

And then he looked at me, and I saw that his eyes were brown. *I got his eyes*, I thought.

I sank into a velvety couch and put my hands out to catch the heat from the fire that burned in a real brick fireplace. The wood made popping sounds as it burned, and a yellow glow filled the whole room.

Winter sat down next to me, and Robert next to her.

"You've really grown up, Winter," he said. I wanted him to say something about me, but he kept his eyes on Winter, on her hair, her face, her hands. Winter wouldn't look at him, though, and kept her eyes locked on the fire.

She tried to speak, but hardly anything came out. A few silent moments passed before she turned to me and said, "Star, tell Dad about your club."

And then he was looking at me, so I sat up as straight as I could and told him about the Emily Dickinson Club, leaving out a few parts that were embarrassing, such as the number of people in it. "I wish a few more people would join," I told him instead.

"Are all your friends already in it?" he asked.

"Yeah," I lied.

"Well," he said, "not everyone likes Emily Dickinson, I guess. Don't worry about it, because you don't want them in your club anyway. They'd just bring the whole thing down, don't you think?"

It wasn't quite the answer I was hoping for. I still wanted more people to join, but I didn't want to hurt his feelings. And it was probably very good advice for a fifth-grader who actually had friends.

He smiled at me, and I was glad I hadn't said anything, because when he smiled, that whole Ferris wheel came to a screeching halt. Both my feet were on the ground, and I realized that this whole time I'd been a little scared—scared that he would be exactly how Mom said he was. Deadbeat, uncaring, not even able to remember our names or birthdays, busy with more important things like his new wife.

Then Winter said, "I'm pregnant."

And his smile evaporated. "Pregnant?" he half whispered. "How?"

"You're pregnant?" I said. Her stomach didn't look any bigger than usual. She looked tiny in the glow of the fire, smaller than Mom after she'd talked to the landlord.

Then he asked her, "What are you going to do?"

It was not at all the reaction Mom would have had. Mom would've screamed, then shrunk down to half her size. "How could you be so stupid?" she'd say. No, not that, because that's what she'd said after Winter's principal called her, and this was an even bigger deal.

I didn't know what Mom would do if she found out.

Winter was still looking at the fire, but her eyes were flat. The fire reflected in them, but she wasn't seeing anything. "I dunno," she said, in answer to Robert's question.

"Have you told anybody?"

"Yeah. You."

He stood up, his hand around Winter's arm. "Come here. Let's go talk about this . . . somewhere else." He said the last two words with his head turned my way. Maybe he thought I was too young to understand, but my fourth-grade teacher had told us about how girls get pregnant. And even if she hadn't, Gloria had given me a rundown the year before at a Heavenly Donuts while Mom took Winter out to buy maxi pads and new underwear.

I stayed on the couch until they left the room, closing the door behind them, and then I followed. Whatever they were saying, I needed to hear it so I could push away the worry forming between my ribs. Would Winter ever be able to leave Sarah Borne if she was pregnant? What if she had to drop out of school completely, like Mom?

Mom said she had lost everyone when she was pregnant. Her parents, who kicked her out of their trailer, and her college friends, who stopped talking to her once she left school, and even the other people in her old trailer park, who called her horrible names and told her she had ruined her life.

All Mom had left was Gloria. But Winter didn't have anyone like Gloria.

She just had me. And what could I do?

Winter and Robert talked in low, low voices out in the hallway. Even with my ear pressed against the door, I couldn't make out what they were saying. After a minute their footsteps began thudding back toward the living room, so I raced back to my spot on the couch and straightened my skirt out.

The door opened. "Ready to go?" Winter asked.

I wasn't ready, but Winter's eyes told me that it wasn't a question. Robert, with his hand on Winter's shoulder, wasn't saying anything.

I got up and followed Winter to the door, digging my toes into the carpet so I could feel its softness one last time and remember it forever. Robert walked us to the front door, staying in his nice, warm house while we stepped out onto the cold, wet porch.

There was still so much I wanted to say to him, about the club and about the Ferris wheel. Had he even known I was up there when he saw Winter all those years ago? But instead, I said, "Will you send me a card for my birthday?" He peered at me, so I added, in case he had forgotten, "It's in July. July ninth."

"You want me to send you a birthday card?" He said it like the idea made no sense. Like he didn't even know what birthdays were.

"You sent Winter one," I told him. "I can wait until I'm thirteen, if you want."

Not one bit of confusion left his face. "Well, sure, Star. I guess I could do that. But Winter's my daughter," he said. "That's why I sent her a birthday card."

"But I am, too," I said. How could he have forgotten *that*? I thought maybe Winter had scrambled up his brain when she told him she was pregnant.

"Oh, no," he said. His eyebrows sagged. "Is that what your mother told you?"

The wind cut into my skin, sapping away all the warmth from the fire. I knew what he was saying before he said it, but I couldn't make myself speak or move. I could only stare up at him and hope that he wouldn't say what he was about to.

"Star," he said. "I'm not your father."

And, piece by aching piece, the Ferris wheel fell completely apart.

CHAPTER 31

It was a long drive back to California.

Rain cascaded down the windshield as the sky grew darker and darker, and with every bump in the road, my bag thudded against my legs. Winter kept rubbing at her eyes, but I didn't bother, because it wasn't like I was going to just stop crying.

After a while, though, my tears slowed, and I was able to choke out the words going around and around in my head. "Who do you think my dad is?"

"I don't know, Star," Winter said.

"I bet Gloria knows," I told her. "Best friends tell each other everything. I bet Mom told her."

Winter stared silently at the road. Her hands gripped

the steering wheel tightly, like if she didn't hold on, she'd fall right out of the pickup.

I watched the droplets on the windshield, grouped together like little puddles. They'd found one another, while I had just splattered on the cement. A cold feeling of loneliness was spreading out from my chest. I wondered if Winter felt the same way.

"What are you going to do?" I asked her, because I certainly didn't know what I was going to do.

"Dad gave me—" She paused, then started again. "*Robert* gave me some money."

"For what?"

"I don't know yet," Winter answered, and her grip on the wheel slackened. "Anything could happen . . ."

But I did not think anything could happen. Hope is not a Ferris wheel, I decided at that moment, because instead of getting closer to Dad, I'd gotten farther and farther away. And unlike a Ferris wheel, which would bring me back around again, this time I was stalled at the top.

Maybe hope is a Gravitron. It looks fun at first—until you're inside, and it's spinning so fast, your head pounds. Then the ride ends, and you vomit. And when you get off the ride, you can't even walk because you're so dizzy, and nothing looks right anymore.

"Star," Winter said after a while. "You have to stop crying." I sniffed, waiting for Winter to put her arm around my shoulders or tell me that things would get better. "Mom will know something's wrong if you go into the trailer crying. We saw the redwoods today, remember?" She tightened her fingers around the steering wheel, her knuckles turning white. "That's all we did."

I checked my bag to see if I'd packed any tissues, but there were none. Just Eddie's big red book and all my starred school papers. For a few miles I thought about saving them. Maybe someday I would meet my real dad, and I could show them to him.

But I pushed that thought away, out of my head. It was all built on a bunch of hope, and I didn't have any of that left.

So after I dried my face with those papers, I ripped them into confetti.

CHAPTER 32

The trailer was heavy with the smell of hamburger. It hit me all at once when we walked in, and I wanted to gag. No wonder Winter was a vegetarian.

"Hi, girls," Mom said. She stood by the stove, stirring a pot, her apron strings dangling at her sides. "I'm making spaghetti sauce. But, Winter, there's a couple cans of tomato soup in the cupboard if you want that instead."

"I'm going to take a nap," Winter said, to me, or Mom. Or the trailer. The mattress creaked as she climbed onto her bed, and I didn't know where to go. I was lost inside the trailer. I almost took a step toward Mom, almost went over and tied her apron for her.

But I didn't.

Because what I'd realized between Oregon and California was that Mom had lied to me. She had been lying to me my whole life. She had convinced me that I wanted to be on that Ferris wheel so that I would never, ever find out that she'd lied.

"Mom," I said.

"What, Star?" she said without turning around.

But I couldn't say anything. I wanted to pull the truth right out of her, say something mean and horrible, something that would hurt her. But I couldn't, because then Mom would know that we hadn't gone to see the redwoods. My throat burned, having to swallow those words.

"What, Star?" Mom said again.

"Nothing," I said. That word came so quickly and easily, but it left a bitter, battery-like taste in my mouth. "I'm . . . not hungry." These words came easily, too, and I knew Mom would be a little hurt that she'd spent so much time making a delicious spaghetti sauce that her daughter did not want to eat.

But it was a very little hurt compared to what I felt.

CHAPTER 33

I spent all Sunday with a headache, a headache that didn't actually hurt. My head just throbbed with the memory of Robert's house and how close I'd been to having a dad before it all fell away. Now I was back to having nothing—not even a PS at the end of a birthday card.

And Winter was back to not talking to anyone, and now that included me, too. Not that I could have talked to her about anything I needed to, since Mom was always in the trailer. Still, I wasn't sure if Winter had stopped talking to me because she was sad about being pregnant or because now she knew I was only her *half* sister. Which doesn't make sense, because I didn't feel any different about Winter, except maybe sadder because I'm not fully related to my favorite person in the world.

But thinking about how much Denny hates his half brother, I wondered if maybe Winter felt differently now, too.

It seemed that way when she breezed out of the trailer Monday morning without a word or even a look.

While I shoveled soggy cereal into my mouth, and Mom and Gloria talked over donuts, I decided that I did not want to go to school. I did not want to sit at my desk or talk to anyone or watch Mr. Savage scratch his beard. I didn't want to pretend that I still cared about the Emily Dickinson Club.

So I told Mom I didn't feel well.

"Do you have a fever?"

"No."

"Does your stomach hurt?"

"No."

"Then go get dressed."

I stuffed my high-tops into my backpack along with all the papers and binders and books that I wasn't even sure why I had anymore, and I left. I took a very small detour on the way to school, to a dead-end street with only two houses on it, one of which was for sale. It took me about ten tries, but I finally managed to throw the high-tops so that they wrapped around a telephone wire.

The closer I got to school, the more I didn't want to be there, and the slower my steps got. I was only two blocks away when my feet just stopped.

Eventually the morning bell rang, but I still didn't move.

I don't know how long it was before I started walking back to the trailer, since I don't have a watch or a cell phone, but I knew it couldn't be 11:00 yet, so when I got to the Treasure Trailers entrance, I snuck behind the tinfoil man's trailer. His tinfoil blinds shifted a bit, but he didn't come out, so I sat down and waited for Gloria's car to go cruising by.

Gloria drove off a few minutes later, with Mom in the passenger seat. When I walked in the door, the clock above the stove read 11:05, which meant Gloria was late for work, and everyone in Mr. Savage's class was going to PE.

Since I wasn't in school, I decided I should try to learn something. So I took out my club notebook and reread some of the Emily Dickinson poems I'd written down all those weeks ago. Maybe she mentioned hope somewhere else and gave it a more accurate description. I was in the middle of "I heard a Fly buzz when I died," when I heard the truck tearing across the gravel and then pulling into our designated driveway.

A few seconds later Winter walked in, jumping when she saw me at the table. "What are you doing here?" she asked.

"I cut school," I told her.

"Oh." She kicked off her combat boots. "Me, too."

This was the first time I'd ever heard of Winter cutting school, but when I told her that, she said, "I do it all the time."

"Really?"

"Yes, really. Don't act so surprised." She tore open the refrigerator door and began pulling out all sorts of things: cucumber, horseradish, cream cheese. I caught the loaf of bread she tossed me and set it on the table for her, then watched her make the world's most disgusting sandwich.

"Didn't you have your club today?" she asked.

"No," I said. "I mean, yes. But I'm gonna cancel it." I'd only just decided that, but once I said it, I felt a little lighter. Like I'd been trying so hard the whole time to start a good club and make some actual friends, when all along I shouldn't have been trying at all.

I half expected Winter to talk me out of it, but she just said, "Good," and took a bite of her sandwich. She must have felt the same way.

"What do you think I should do about Dad?" I asked, thinking maybe she'd have a good answer to that. Her mouth was full, so she had to finish chewing before she answered.

"I dunno," she said, and then took another bite.

"Do you think I should try to find him somehow?"

"Star," she said, spewing little chunks of food across the table, "I don't know, okay? I don't even know what *I'm* doing. Can't you just figure something out on your own for once?"

Her words made me wince. Not just the words but the way she said them—like she was absolutely sick of me. I wanted to apologize, but I wasn't sure what to apologize for.

The phone rang, and Winter jumped up to grab it. "Hello?" she answered. "Yes, this is Carly Mackie." Winter narrowed her eyes at me, and I squeezed my hands together in my lap. "Yes, she's home sick. I'm sorry I forgot to call. Good-bye." She hung up the phone and told me, "Don't cut school anymore. You're gonna get both of us in trouble."

She finished her sandwich in silence, then stomped out of the trailer without saying good-bye. I listened to the truck peeling out of the lot, thinking that Emily Dickinson's poem should have been about loneliness instead of hope, because that's what was perching in my soul. No Mom, no Dad, no friends, and now, no Winter.

I didn't have a single person left.

CHAPTER 34

I threw out all the Emily Dickinson poems and cut up my club notebook with heavy-duty scissors. As I tossed all the strips of notebook into the dumpster, I thought about what I was going to do next. What I had to do, since Mom wouldn't tell me the truth.

I went back to the trailer and stood in front of Mom's door. She never locks it, so I went right in and started looking around for the key to the shed, opening drawers and being careful to smooth out the clothes inside so she'd never know I was in there.

I found the key in Mom's nightstand, hidden under a framed photo of Winter and me. Winter was six in the picture, maybe seven, and I was a baby. She was holding me, trying to lift me up off the ground.

Winter was right. I was too old now for her to pick me up, for her to have to keep helping. I was going to figure this out on my own and solve my own problems for once.

I snuck out of the trailer, even though I knew Mom wouldn't be home anytime soon, because everyone in our row at Treasure Trailers is a big gossip, according to Gloria. The shed was in an empty lot behind the landlord's house, with a bunch of other sheds. It took a few tries before I found the right one.

I started to go through boxes and trash bags. Under a box of photos, and under a box marked ASSORTED WIGS, was the IMPORTANT STUFF box. I opened it up and began looking. I checked every single scrap of paper, even things that would never have my dad's name on them, like the invoices from our last dentist visit three years ago. (Cavities are expensive.)

I found out a lot of things looking through that box, like where all the Food Bank cards had disappeared to. I was beginning to think that maybe Mom had been really serious about keeping Dad a complete secret. But then I found Winter's birth certificate, and there on the same line as *Name of father* was *Robert Carlisle*. So I stopped looking at every tiny scrap and started looking for my birth certificate.

It wasn't much farther down.

Name of child: Star Bright Mackie. That was me. I used to hate my middle name until I found out Winter's is Gloria.

Name of mother: Carlotta Janine Mackie.

And then, *Name of father: Francis Tangelo.*

I could have been Star Tangelo. Or Star Mackie-Tangelo. Or Star Tangelo-Mackie. It was hard to decide which one was best, since they were all better than plain old Star Mackie, but I probably would have liked Star Tangelo, because then nobody would have called me Star Trashy.

I checked outside, and it wasn't dark yet, so I still had a bit more time to snoop around. I dug through the rest of the box, and there, almost at the very, very bottom, I found it.

An envelope. Mom's name was right there in the center, and there was no letter inside, but that didn't matter. The date on the stamp was from seven years ago, but that didn't matter either. What mattered was the address in the upper left corner of the envelope, under the name Frank Tangelo.

My father's address.

CHAPTER 35

Dear Dad,

This is your daughter, Star Mackie. I'm ten years old now and in fifth grade. My teacher is horrible, and I hate him. The boy who sits in front of me is also horrible, and I hate him, too. I would have written you a letter much sooner, but Mom wouldn't tell me who you were.

I just want to know a few things:

1. If you knew it was my birthday, would you send me a birthday card? If you already know my birthday, why didn't you send me one? Is it because of Mom? Because I don't care what she says anymore. (My birthday is July 9, by the way.)

2. Did you know I have a sister? I think you should know, because Winter (my sister) has a different father, and he knows all about me. I even got to meet him. Weird, huh? Maybe we should meet, too!

3. Do you have brown eyes?

4. What is a club I could start that everyone would actually want to join? I have already tried the Trailer Park Club and the Emily Dickinson Club, but they aren't working.

5. When Mom was pregnant with me, did she eat disgusting things? Like cucumber and horseradish sandwiches? I would ask Mom, but I think I'm not going to talk to her for a while.

Hope you are doing well.

Love, your daughter,
Star Mackie

CHAPTER 36

It was the easiest letter in the world to write. In fact, I could have written more, but I didn't want the envelope to be too heavy or for him to get bored while reading it and decide that maybe he'd rather be eating a grilled cheese sandwich or something.

I had it stamped and ready to go and dropped it into the collection box down the street. Hope was beginning to spin again, and when I woke up the next morning, my head wasn't throbbing anymore and I didn't feel like spending another entire day at Treasure Trailers, so I got dressed and ate a piece of peanut butter bread on my way to school.

I got there early enough to have to drop my backpack

off by Mr. Savage's door. Some of the girls from class were there, folding fortune-tellers from a big stack of old homework assignments. I tried to shoo away the loneliness that came to perch, and I finally just walked away.

I made my way to the playground, to the bench by the United States map, to wait for the bell to ring. But the second I sat down, Eddie appeared, his feet planted right in the middle of California. "Where were you yesterday?" he asked.

"Sick," I said. I wondered if I should cough or something, but I didn't bother.

"Oh," he said, sitting down next to me. "'Cause you never showed up for club, and Langston and I sat there like fools for, like, a half hour before Miss Fergusson said it was obvious no one was coming."

Denny and Genny weren't even there? I guess they knew I was sick, so they hadn't shown up. "Sorry," I told Eddie.

"That's okay," he said, and he spit on the ground. "Miss Fergusson says we can have her room today. Are we still gonna read something by Emily Dickinson, or did you find any better poems?"

"I . . ." I didn't know what to say. "I don't . . ."

Sighing, Eddie leaned back and stretched his long legs.

"If you really want to do Emily Dickinson again, that's fine."

The bell rang, and I didn't move.

Eddie didn't either.

I was still ready to cancel the whole club, but now, with my letter on the way to Dad, the Ferris wheel was slowly piecing itself back together. Hope was starting to make its way around again, and I figured I could at least have one more meeting.

As the monitors blew their whistles and pulled kids off the jungle gym so they could line up for class, I told Eddie I'd see him after school in Miss Fergusson's room.

I was even sort of excited.

CHAPTER 37

Genny sat next to me at lunch, planting her organic pudding in the empty slot on my lunch tray. "It's too bad you were sick yesterday," Genny said. "The lady from the art museum came in and showed us how to draw bats."

It would have been nice to know how to draw a bat, but otherwise I didn't feel that I'd missed very much. Genny asked what I was going to be for Halloween, which was on Friday. I took an extra big bite of pudding so I wouldn't have to say that I had kind of forgotten.

"I want to be a bird warrior woman," Genny told me, "but we don't have enough feathers. Or enough glue. And

Mom says I can't glue feathers on my head." It didn't seem to bother her that much. Nothing ever bothered Genny. It must be nice, I thought, right as Genny said, "I wonder what Eddie will dress up as."

"You can ask him after school," I said as Denny sat down, sliding a chocolate milk into Genny's waiting hand.

"It's Tuesday," he said, and he gave me his most serious glare.

"Miss Fergusson said we could use her room today, since I was gone yesterday." I couldn't help smiling as Denny ripped the top off his milk. "It was Eddie's idea."

"We have to go home," Denny said. "We don't live in a trailer park, so our parents actually want us to come home after school."

I was building up a couple of choice words when Genny spoke up. "We just have to text Mom, that's all. Text her after school."

But there was no way Denny was going to do that, so I suggested that Genny text her mom herself. "I can't," she told me. "I don't have a phone anymore. I kept losing it. Denny's the responsible one." It sounded like a compliment, but Denny shook his head, scowling.

I should have asked in my letter if Dad has a cell phone. Not that I could text him, since I don't have one, but at least then I could call sometimes. I made a mental note to put it in my next letter. And another mental note to find out how long it takes for mail to go from California to Oregon.

CHAPTER 38

The rest of the day dragged on and on, and Mr. Savage, who was in some kind of beard-scratching frenzy, made us read about the *Mayflower* straight from our history books. When I was learning about the Oregon Trail back in Oregon, everyone in class got to play a game in the computer lab. But we only have one computer in Mr. Savage's class, and it's brand-brand-new and doesn't have any games on it. Also, no one ever made a game about the *Mayflower*, and if they did, it would probably be really boring.

When the bell finally rang, and we finally got to Miss Fergusson's room, and everyone but the five of us had finally cleared out, we moved our desks together in their usual circle and sat down.

No one said a word. They were all waiting for me. Eddie with his arms crossed, Langston with his feet on the desk, Denny with a mile-long glare, and Genny with her pencil poised and ready to take minutes. Even Miss Fergusson, at her desk, was looking up at me from her grade book.

I reached into my backpack and felt around for at least ten seconds before I remembered that I had ripped all the pages out of my club notebook. "Oh," I said. "I don't have any poems with me."

From her desk, Miss Fergusson called out, "You want me to print you some?"

"Uh, no," I decided. "Today . . . Eddie's gonna take over."

Langston started laughing, then stopped when Eddie shoved him out of his chair. "You want me to lead?" Eddie asked. "What poem are we doing?"

"You get to decide," I told him. "It's your choice."

"*Any* poem?"

"Any poem." I figured that'd shut him up for a while.

He thought for a moment before rushing over to Miss Fergusson. After a few clicks of her mouse and some quick typing, her printer began spitting out a page, which Eddie then grabbed and brought back to the group.

"Here," he said, slapping the sheet of paper onto Denny's desk. "Do something for a change."

Denny scowled, but his fear of being punched must have won out, because he began to read.

Hold fast to dreams
For if dreams die
Life is a broken-winged bird
That cannot fly.

"Wing-ed," Eddie corrected. "It has to be two syllables, otherwise it won't sound right."

Denny continued.

Hold fast to dreams
For when dreams go
Life is a barren field
Frozen with snow.

It was beautiful and short and reminded me of Emily Dickinson, except not as old-fashioned.

"I think this poem is a better version of Emily Dickinson's poem about hope," Eddie told us.

"And," Genny said, scribbling in the minutes, "they're both about birds."

I didn't say anything. I wasn't going to argue that Emily Dickinson's version was still better, because I didn't think I had to.

"That's true," Eddie said. "And also, Emily Dickinson said hope *perches,* but in this poem, dreams can *fly.*"

"Who wrote it?" Genny asked. Her pencil hovered above her paper, ready to write down the name.

"Langston Hughes," Eddie told us.

Heavenly Donuts. There was no way. I turned to Langston and said, "You wrote that?" He smiled at me until Eddie informed us all, through a fit of laughter, that Langston couldn't write a grocery list. Langston Hughes was some other guy, a famous poet who was, like Emily Dickinson, dead.

"Oh." I remembered. "So *you're* the one named after the famous poet."

"Someday people will say that he was named after me," Langston insisted.

This time both Denny and Eddie rolled their eyes.

We talked a bit more, mostly about the difference between dreams and hope, which we eventually agreed were basically the same thing. Because, as we had to remind Langston, the dreams mentioned in the poems were not the dreams you have when you go to sleep. "We should do what we did before," Eddie said, "when we said what hope was. But this time we can replace it with *dreams*. We'll see if they're still the same."

"Metaphors," Miss Fergusson called out from her desk. Her head was still buried in her grade book, but her voice carried across the room. "When you compare one thing to another thing by saying they're the same, even though they actually aren't, that's a metaphor. That's what you were doing last week."

"I knew that," Eddie called back to her. "Anyway, I said hope was a rock," he told us. "And I still think that applies to dreams. And the more I've thought about it, the less stupid it sounds."

It was Denny's turn next, but he just said, "Pass."

Langston said he'd forgotten what he'd said about hope in the first place, but after Genny reminded him that he'd talked about a dirty window, he chewed on his fingernail and thought. "Dreams are different," he said, finally. "Dreams can be clean windows. You can see through them better, but the glass is still in the way."

Genny made us wait while she wrote hers down:

Dreams. Alive, but dead.

They can't breathe or blink, I think.

They live in your head.

Another haiku?

"So, Star. Do you think dreams can be a Ferris wheel?" Genny asked.

I wasn't sure. "I think dreams are different," I said. I thought about it for a minute, and that's when I got it. "Dreams are a letter," I said. "You fill it with all your thoughts and feelings and wishes. But then you have to send it away, and you're not sure when it will get where it's going or if you'll get anything back at all. But you have to send it to find out."

Eddie was looking smug over at his desk, but I thought my answer was the best.

Once Genny finished up with the minutes, we ended the meeting and moved the desks back into their regular formation before heading outside. It was colder now, so we all stood around putting on our jackets. "That was fun," Genny said. "No offense, Star, but sometimes Emily Dickinson makes me sleepy."

I tried my best to not look as offended as I felt.

Eddie told me he had a whole bunch of new poem ideas to share for our meeting next week, too. He was practically grinning, and he looked like a completely different person. A person who had never punched anyone in his life. "No Robert Frost," he was saying. "We're gonna stay away from that fool for as long as we can."

What was he talking about? "This is the Emily Dickinson Club," I reminded everyone.

"Well, today it was more like the Langston Hughes Club," Genny said, reading from the minutes.

"It's the Emily Dickinson Club," I said again. "We can't go changing it now. Besides, if we did, then Eddie would have to run it." I didn't know nearly as much about poetry as Eddie did, but I was pretty sure I knew more than he did about Emily Dickinson.

"What if we take turns?" Eddie asked, stepping closer to me. Still grinning, like he wasn't trying to take over the club.

I looked over at Genny to see what she thought and caught her adding to the minutes. "Don't put this in," I told her.

"It seems important," she said.

"It's not important, because Eddie is not in charge, so he doesn't get to make any decisions," I said. I turned back to Eddie and found that his smile had vanished.

"You're so stubborn," he said, pushing past me. "C'mon, Langston." And the two of them stalked off. Well, only Eddie stalked. Langston strolled along beside him.

"Whatever," Denny said, when Langston and Eddie were out of sight. "This club would suck no matter what it was about."

"Denny!" Surprisingly, Genny's face turned bright red. "Don't be such a crab!"

"It's the truth," Denny said, glaring right at me. "Why do you think nobody wants to be in your stupid club? It's not because of Emily Dickinson. It's because of *you*. No one likes *you*." Then he turned to go. "Come on, Genny. This club's over."

I'd already known that Denny hated me. And I guess I'd known that no one else in class really liked me either, since they hadn't stopped calling me Star Trashy. But it still hurt to hear it said out loud.

"I like the club," Genny said.

"It doesn't matter," I said. "I mean, he's right. It's not like we'll ever get anyone else to join. This club is just a waste of time." I sighed, trying to keep myself from crying. "Plus, now Eddie hates me, too." If only I hadn't sent my letter to Dad already. Maybe he could have told me what to do.

Genny was seething next to me. Denny's words had nested in my throat, but they'd just made Genny mad. "He's wrong. Okay, Star? You'll see. Don't worry. " She ran after her brother.

I wanted to believe her, but Denny was right.

Nobody liked Star Trashy.

Star Mackie

October 30

Week 7 Vocabulary Sentences

Why am I still doing these?

1. I am desperate to talk to Winter, or anyone else even, but preferably Winter, because she's the best at telling me that things will get better and how to make sure that they do.
2. I would even accept a Winter doppelganger. (And a Mr. Savage doppelganger, as long as he did not assign weird words.)
3. Plus, it'd be nice to know that Winter is okay. I can't even fathom what she's thinking—partly because she won't tell me, and partly because it's too hard to imagine.
4. It kind of sucks when you have no one else to talk to. It also sucks when half your club mates hate you, and it's not like you can induce anyone else to join your club, because they don't like you either.
5. Especially when they're all too busy jeering at you. And after a while, it's too easy to think that they're right.

6. Mostly I just want a letter from Dad to arrive, because I feel like I'm standing at the <u>margin</u> of hope, and the longer the letter takes, the closer I get to the very edge.
7. Or like I'm on a Ferris wheel that won't stop turning, and there's this <u>ominous</u> feeling, like if I don't get off soon, it'll be too late.
8. I wish hope was more like a <u>rampart</u>, something I could build up to protect myself when bad things happen. That would be a lot more useful than something that just perches there, waiting, or spins, sometimes without stopping.
9. The waiting is the worst part. I'd feel <u>substantially</u> better if there was no waiting at all. I'd even feel <u>substantially</u> better if I had anyone to talk to, but I think that, even if I did, they wouldn't understand.
10. So I guess the reason I'm still doing these sentences, even though I'm not very <u>zealous</u> about them, is because I have no one to talk to but myself. And that's better than nothing.

CHAPTER 39

Detention shifted to Thursday this week so that no one would have to stay after school on Halloween. How nice.

Just kidding. It was terrible. But not because something horrible happened. I was just ready to get the heck out of there and check the mail. I knew it had only been three days since I'd sent that letter to Dad, but maybe that had been enough time for the letter to have gotten there and for a letter to come back.

So I was focusing on the letter and not on detention, because detention is always the same anyway. That's why it took me so long to notice that Eddie wasn't there. Which was odd. I'd always thought he was kind of a permanent fixture. After detention, I asked Miss Fergusson if he was sick that day.

"No, no," Miss Fergusson told me. "He turned in all his overdue work, so he doesn't have detention anymore. Ever since he joined your club, he's been doing a lot better in class."

Great. Miss Fergusson looked so happy, I didn't know how to tell her that Eddie hated me now, and the club was over. If only he was in detention, I could have apologized. "Do you think Eddie's better at running the club than me?" I asked Miss Fergusson.

"I think, Miss Star Mackie, that without you, Eddie would be failing the fifth grade, as smart as he is. That's what I think." She smiled at me and gave me a butterscotch candy from her desk.

It's so unfair that I'm stuck with Mr. Savage all year.

I thanked Miss Fergusson and left. And instead of having Eddie next to me, all I had was stupid loneliness, perching and laughing. I even missed Eddie's stupid poems.

As I headed past Mrs. Feinstein's room, a big crowd of fourth-grade detention junkies flooded out, and among them were some very familiar tattooed arms.

"Hi!" Genny said, dragging two girls over with her. One was tall and the other short, and they both stared at the fringes of my hair. "This is Maggie and Chelsea. They said they'd join the Emily Dickinson Club."

"Oh." I was too surprised to say anything else.

"We said we'd check it out," said Maggie or Chelsea. I didn't know who was who.

"Who's Emily Dickinson?" the other one said. "An actress or something?"

"We meet on Mondays," Genny told them, pushing them along on their way. They walked down the hallway without a backward glance. "See?" Genny told me. "I told you Denny was wrong."

"What are you doing in detention?" I asked.

"Well, I don't have lunch at the same time as the other fourth-graders," she said. "And I had to talk to them to see if they'd join the club. Plus, I wanted to see Mrs. Feinstein's pinkie. She really does keep it in her desk!" Her eyes grew wide. "It's so gross-looking. It looks like a dried-up pickle."

I still didn't understand. "How did you even get detention?"

Turns out it was a two-day ordeal. The day before, she'd kicked a ball over the fence, thrown a bunch of wet paper towels on the ceiling in the girls' bathroom, and then, for good measure, she hadn't turned in her sentences today.

"Detention's kind of fun," she finished.

Detention was not fun. "You just sit there, and you

can't talk to anyone," I said. "And everyone's extra mean, because they're all delinquents-in-training."

"Well, then, why are you in detention?" she asked. "Anyway, this is great! Now we can be detention buddies. Hi, Langston."

She said the last two words to Langston, who had been standing right behind me for I didn't want to know how long.

"Hi, Genny," he said. "Mullet." That was to me, obviously. "Here, I have something for you. Proof that I am the superior Langston." And from his pocket he pulled out a tiny, folded-up piece of paper and practically shoved it into my hands. The folds were so small and tight, it took a long time to open it all the way, and when I finally did, I saw only four lines:

Roses are red
Mullets are blue
Poems are stupid
Admit it, it's true.

"Wow," I said. "This is a terrible poem."

"Are you joking? I spent all day on that!"

"Let me see!" Genny insisted, but Langston shook his head so hard, just watching it made my neck hurt.

"It's for Star," he told her, and then to me, he said, "I thought girls liked poems."

I wouldn't exactly consider it a poem, but sure, girls like poems. For a moment I wondered why we didn't have more girls in the club. Genny and I were outnumbered by boys. The moment ended when I noticed Langston staring at me. Just sunken-eyed staring.

And right when I was on the verge of telling him how creepy that was, he said, "Well, see ya, Mullet." And he jogged away.

I kind of forgot that Genny was still there, so when she tapped me on the shoulder, my body jerked like a stalling truck. We walked out to the front entrance together, where Denny was apparently waiting for us. Well, for Genny. Like he'd ever wait for me.

He did glare at me, though, even while he told Genny it was time to go. Genny smiled at me and said she couldn't wait for detention next Friday.

"You won't be in detention next Friday," Denny told her.

"Sure, I will," she said. "I hardly got to talk to anyone. Did you know I got us two new club members today? I bet I'll get more next—"

"Genny." That was all he had to say, and Genny stopped talking.

But I didn't want Genny thinking that she'd done something wrong, just because her jerk of a brother didn't like it. "Thanks, Genny. You really did prove him wrong." Although it wasn't true. I'm sure Chelly and Mags, or whatever their names were, didn't actually like me and therefore wouldn't like the club.

Denny didn't like that one bit, though. "You shut up," he snapped. "If it weren't for you, she wouldn't even be in detention." And he left, pulling his sister behind him.

I stood there for a while before remembering that Langston and Eddie were gone, so I didn't have anybody waiting with me, and I could just go. So I trudged home to Treasure Trailers. And checked the mailbox. And trudged to the trailer, empty-handed.

Not counting that terrible poem, of course.

CHAPTER 40

I probably would have dressed up for Halloween if Mom hadn't said anything. But when I woke up Friday morning and Mom cheerfully asked if I was going to wear my lawyer costume from last year, I couldn't say anything other than "No." I wanted to see her face fall in disappointment, the way mine had when Robert told me he wasn't my father.

"Well, we never got a chance to go costume shopping this year," Mom said. "Sorry about that."

Sorry about a dumb costume? *That's* what she was sorry about? I put on the most ordinary clothes I owned. Then I changed, just in case people thought I was dressing up as Normal Girl or something.

Winter was already gone when I left. She was always leaving early and coming back late, and then she'd spend all her trailer time in her bed, reading or doing homework or just lying there and staring at the ceiling. Gloria said Winter was in one of her moods again, but I knew the real reason she wouldn't talk to us.

I wanted her to talk to me about being pregnant. And I wanted to talk to her about my letter to Dad and the club and everything else. It was nice knowing that Dad would send a letter back soon, but problems were starting to pop up all over the place, and even though Winter had told me to solve them on my own, it'd be great if she could give me a couple of hints.

On the way to school I checked the mail, even though I knew it wouldn't get there until afternoon. And, just as I thought, there wasn't anything in there but a dead earwig.

Since it was Halloween, we didn't do any actual work at school, and the whole day was kind of like a party, even for the two people who didn't dress up—Denny and me. Genny, in a sweaterdress with feathers glued all over it, told me that Denny was too old to dress up.

"What about Allie?" I asked.

"He's a troll," Genny said.

I didn't know if she meant that was his costume, but I didn't ask.

"What's Winter?" she asked.

Luckily we had to sit down then, and I didn't have to admit that I had no idea if Winter had even dressed up.

Mr. Savage kept me in during recess, as always. I thought he'd cut me some slack, since it was Halloween, but I guess not. Once everyone was gone, I headed over to the sink to fill the bucket so I could wash desks, since that was my usual job. But Mr. Savage called me up to his desk before I could turn on the water.

"So," he said.

I waited, watching in disgust as his hand went straight for his beard.

"I heard you started a new club in Miss Fergusson's room." He leaned back in his chair. "The Emily Dickinson Club. What a great idea for a club."

Mr. Savage hates me and would never give me a compliment. I knew this had to be a trick, so I didn't say a thing.

"Unfortunately, I haven't received your sentences yet," he continued. "So you're going to have to cancel your club."

I remembered having arguments ready in case Mr. Savage discovered the club, but I couldn't remember exactly what they were. So again, I didn't say anything. I just let the hollow feeling in my stomach creep its way into my chest.

"When you bring me your sentences, we can talk about whether or not to reinstate your club," Mr. Savage said, along with some other things I didn't listen to. I was too busy thinking that I should have just handed the club over to Eddie while I had the chance.

I shuddered, remembering how mad Eddie had been on Tuesday. Mad enough . . . to tell Mr. Savage that I had illegally moved and renamed my club? Mad enough to get it taken away forever?

I felt sick. And I had to stand there and pretend to listen to Mr. Savage's rotten speech for the whole recess and not cry and not grab the glass apple off his desk and pitch it through the window, and it was maybe the hardest thing I'd ever had to do, but I got through it. I got through it, and during the Halloween Parade after lunch, which was just everyone walking on the painted track that looped around the playground, I found Eddie.

He hadn't dressed up either.

"The club got canceled," I told him, and he said, "I know." Which just confirmed what I already suspected.

"I know you know!" I said, as we passed a couple of slow-walking fourth-graders. "Because you *told* Mr. Savage so he'd take my club away and so you could get back at me for not letting you turn it into a Poetry Club!"

"No, I know because Miss Fergusson told me, after

Mr. Savage told her, after somebody told him," he said. "Besides, I would've just socked you if I wanted to get you back for something. I'm not a coward."

Yes, now that I thought about it, getting the club canceled was not something Eddie would have done. "Oh," I said. "Sorry."

"That's okay," Eddie said. "People are always accusing me of things. I'm kind of used to it."

"Well," I said, "Mr. Savage only canceled *my* club. I'm sure you could start your own club. It could even be a Poetry Club."

"Yeah, but then you couldn't join."

"So what? You can run it," I told him, but he shook his brown curls at me.

"Then it'd just be me and Langston," he said. "And Langston would quit once he found out you weren't gonna be there."

I spotted Langston's mohawk up ahead, in a big group of sixth-graders. I couldn't tell if he had a costume on, but he was laughing and shouting with everyone else. "Why? He's your friend."

"Yeah, but he likes *you*." Eddie laughed. "You didn't think he actually liked Emily Dickinson, did you?"

Langston looked back then and saw me and waved, and I focused on my shoes so he wouldn't see how red my face was. I didn't think a boy had ever actually liked me before. And a sixth-grader! Maybe the girls in class would be jealous if I told them. But then they still wouldn't want to be my friends, would they?

"Anyway, I'm not smart enough to run that club," Eddie said. And the weird thing was, he was completely serious.

"What are you talking about? You're the smartest one in the club!" It was maddening, but he was.

"If I was smart, I wouldn't have gotten held back," he said, and he reminded me that he couldn't even read when he was in first grade—both times he was in first grade.

"You can read now," I pointed out, but Eddie just grumbled about how *everyone can read now, Star.*

Yeah, I thought, *everyone reads thousand-page books and has fifty different poems memorized.* "You really don't think you're smart?"

"I know I'm not smart, and everyone else knows it, too. That's why everyone's afraid of me. Because I had to beat people up so much for calling me stupid all the time." As if to prove it, he jerked at a passing sixth-grader, who jumped and started walking the other way. "I can tell they're still thinking it, though. Teachers included."

"I don't think anyone from the club thinks you're stupid," I told him. "Miss Fergusson included."

"Hmph" was all he had to say to that. And then he shoved me, just a little bit, sending me off the track. We didn't say much to each other for the rest of the parade, but I could tell that Eddie didn't hate me anymore, and that was nice.

Of course, I still didn't know how Mr. Savage had found out about the club.

"Hey," Eddie said before we went to line back up. "Genny told me you were upset because there are only five of us in the club."

"Genny talked to you?" I asked. Genny was doing all kinds of weird things lately. First detention, and now this.

"Well, I like having only five people," he told me. "You're new this year, so you don't know that everyone else pretty much sucks."

That made me smile. It was nice to know that even though Eddie didn't like anyone else, he liked me.

Maybe the club had actually worked. Not completely, but a little bit. "You don't think that having only five people makes it a bad club?" I asked.

"We could have four people," Eddie said. "You can kick that Denny kid out, since he just sits there." I pointed out that Langston also just sat there, mostly, and Eddie said, "Yeah, but I like Langston."

"Denny has to stay," I told him. "I think he and Genny

have to be together." What was I talking about? "It doesn't matter anyway. I can't get the club back."

Eddie walked away, shaking his head. "So stubborn," I heard him say.

"So are you," I told him, but he was too far away to hear.

CHAPTER 41

I didn't go trick-or-treating. I did stop by the tinfoil man's trailer with Gloria, because he'd told her he had something he wanted to give me.

It was a toffee bar wrapped in tinfoil.

"Thanks," I told his hand, which was the only thing I saw. It nodded at me and then disappeared back inside his trailer.

Mom made pumpkin soup for dinner, which was awful, and not only because everything Mom cooked lately seemed to taste like ash. It was actually awful, and I never wanted to eat it again. Gloria ended up pouring hers in the toilet. But when Winter came home, she ate the rest of the pot and then asked if there was any more.

"Ha! It wasn't that bad!" Mom said.

But it was. And it seemed like that awful soup sloshed around in my stomach all weekend. Or maybe it was just because I was so anxious about that letter. It didn't come Saturday, and I checked the mail twice on Sunday before remembering that there wasn't any mail on Sundays. I should have remembered that, considering Mom's year-long stint working at the post office back in Brookings.

There still wasn't a letter on Monday morning either. I got to school early and used the library computer to type in *How long does it take for a letter to get from California to Oregon?* But I guess it depended on the cities, because California is a million miles long, and Oregon has all those long stretches full of trees and empty of houses. One website said between two and seven days.

So that was a bust.

I asked the librarian if she had any books about pregnancy or being pregnant. "Is your mother pregnant, dear?" she asked.

"I'm just curious," I said. She gave me a big hardcover, which I took to the bench to read and then promptly wished I hadn't.

Being pregnant sucks.

Pregnant women get sick and throw up, they have crazy mood swings and food cravings, and also, because of carrying a baby around along with a bunch of pregnancy weight, they get horrible back problems.

But the very worst part of the book was the end, where there was a picture of a mother and her newborn baby. The mother looked like she had just run a twenty-mile marathon without drinking any water, and the baby was covered in . . . I didn't even know what.

I returned that book immediately.

No wonder Winter wanted me to solve my own problems, when her problem was so, so huge. And if Mom found out? It'd be even huger.

CHAPTER 42

Even though I went out of my way to choose a spot that was out of everyone else's way, Genny managed to find me in the cafeteria, setting her brown paper bag next to my tray.

"I think Chelsea and Maggie changed their minds," Genny said.

"Really?" I wasn't actually that surprised. "Why do you think that?"

"Well, Chelsea came up to me and said that she and Maggie didn't want to be in the club after all."

Before I could tell Genny that I was thinking maybe the club had been fine the way it was, Denny set his lunch bag down across from us. And when I say *set*, I really mean *slammed*. He dug a dollar bill out of his pocket and slid it over to Genny, saying, "Go buy us some milk."

"Sure!" Genny said, and she skipped off, probably excited to have a very nice conversation with the lunch lady.

Once she was fully embroiled in the milk line, Denny whirled on me and said, "Okay. Enough is enough. You're done hanging out with my sister."

"Yeah, right," I told him. Like I was going to stop talking to the only girl in school who was actually nice to me.

"I'm serious," he said, yanking everything out of his bag and slamming it onto the table. "She can't be around you anymore. You know she's *trying* to get detention again?" He made it sound like detention was the most disgusting thing on the planet. "At home, she's always talking about you and your stupid clothes and how she wants to get a stupid mullet."

"It's a *layered cut,*" I said, which drew the attention of the two nearest tables. "It's supposed to look like this! It's not a mullet!"

He acted like he hadn't heard a single thing I'd said. "She was doing just fine until you came around," he said. "You and your trashy sister."

"Don't you say that about Winter! You don't even know her!"

"I know she came over this weekend begging Allie to get back together with her," he said, and a horrible laugh tumbled out of his mouth. "He turned her down, too. She must be a real loser if she got dumped by Allie. He's the king of losers."

I heard them, all around us—the kids at the other tables, laughing. I was used to Denny glaring at me and saying terrible things, but hearing him bad-mouth Winter was too much.

"You're not in the club anymore," I told him.

"There is *no club!"* he screamed at me, his eyes wide. "I told Mr. Savage what you did, and now it's gone! So leave my sister *alone*."

So it was Denny who'd ratted me out, and now that I looked back on what had happened, I couldn't believe I'd ever thought it could be Eddie. "You're nothing but a dirt-sucking termite," I said. I could have called him a cockroach, because cockroaches are ugly, but termites are ugly *and* they destroy things.

"And you're a trailer-trash freak, just like your sister," he said.

Voices rose around us, from every table—shrieks of every pitch, along with the loud hiss of dozens of whispers, and all of it surrounded by laughter. That poor lunchtime monitor didn't even know where to start shushing.

That's when Genny came back with the milks. "Why were you screaming?" she asked, handing Denny a carton of chocolate milk.

I grabbed it right out of his hand. He was too shocked to do anything, so he just watched as I opened it, on both sides, and then dumped the entire thing over his head.

"Star!" Genny gasped.

"He sold us out!" I told her, but that didn't wipe the horrified expression from her face. I didn't get it. She lived with Denny. She knew what a jerk he was. I bet she wanted to punch him every single day, but she couldn't because they were family.

Then something squished into the side of my head, and I heard a dozen voices around me all say, "Eww!" I reached up and peeled a piece of mayonnaise-covered bread—excuse me, *organic* mayonnaise-covered bread—off of my face.

"Denny!" Genny squeaked, just as he smooshed another piece right onto my forehead.

For the first time, I wished the hot lunch was that horrible beef stroganoff. It would have been the perfect thing to throw. But all I had on my tray was a pizza rectangle.

So I grabbed an applesauce from the kid behind me and flung it right at Denny's head.

And then it got *bad*. Denny got ahold of someone's

macaroni and cheese, and then I got his pants with Jell-O. He threw ranch dressing on me, and then I pushed some kids out of the way to get to the good stuff: salsa, yogurt, noodles, raisins. The whole time, Genny was screaming for us to stop, but Denny wasn't backing down, and neither was I. I was finally getting him back for all the horrible things he'd said and done and glared.

But then two monitors ran up and grabbed our food-stained arms. A third monitor stood in the middle of the cafeteria, blowing so hard on her whistle, her face had turned red.

All around us, the shouts and laughter faded into whispers and then into nothing but staring. I wasn't sure how I looked, but Denny looked bad, with chocolate milk dripping off his bangs. I wiped some mayonnaise out of my hair and onto my skirt, and then the monitors took us away.

We passed Genny, at the end of the table, and she looked like she was about to cry. I was relieved to see that she hadn't gotten any food on her. "I'm sorry," I told her, but I don't think she heard. She was glaring right at Denny, and her glare was a thousand times worse than any of his.

I almost felt bad for him.

CHAPTER 43

After washing up and sitting in the principal's office for half an hour without saying anything, Denny and I finally got sent out into the hallway while the principal called our parents. Parent. Whatever.

The librarian was keeping an eye on us but also reading a picture book to herself. I could've made a break for it and gotten a few blocks away before she noticed. Instead, I slouched against the wall while my butt slowly went numb. I guess chairs were too much to ask for now that we were hardened criminals.

"There's something wrong with you," Denny whispered to me. I didn't bother answering. "You're acting different.

It's like something really horrible must have happened to you or your sister or something."

That was surprising. Out of everyone in the whole school, Denny was the one who'd noticed. I almost took back every horrible thing I'd ever said about him, until he added, "It's pathetic."

The librarian shushed us back into silence.

Denny's mom showed up first—dark-haired and blue-eyed and kind of glare-y, like her son, and with a tattoo on her arm, like her daughter. Denny followed her into the principal's office.

Mom showed up about two minutes later. Obviously she'd been in the middle of getting highlights (to match her lowlights, I guess) because she still had the tinfoil in her hair.

"What is the matter with you?" were the first words out of her mouth. When the librarian shushed her, Mom said, "Are you watching my kid, or are you reading a book? And don't you dare say *both*!" The librarian left her alone after that.

Mom sat down on her heels next to me, but I wouldn't look at her. I only heard her voice—and everything packed inside it: confusion, anger, concern.

"Why are you getting into fights?" she asked, even

though it hadn't even been a real fight. "You're acting like Winter," she said, even though Winter didn't get into any fights, so how was acting like her a bad thing? "You've been so quiet lately. Why aren't you talking to me?" she asked, and I didn't say a single thing.

A minute later, the principal called us in for a conference or something. I don't think either Denny or I was listening, and we still weren't saying anything.

At one point I heard Denny's mom say, "This is just so abnormal for him," which made me laugh out loud. The whole office was silent while she glared at me.

The meeting ended with both our moms agreeing that Denny and I would write apology letters to each other. I guess since the principal couldn't get us to talk, he'd make us write. If Denny's eye-roll was any indication, he thought this was as dumb an idea as I did.

Oh, and we were dismissed for the day, which was better than being suspended or expelled, I guess.

"Honestly, Star," Mom said, walking through the parking lot with her fists jammed into her pockets, "you and your sister are really testing my patience right now. I can't believe you would do this to me. What if you'd been expelled?"

I didn't think anyone had ever been expelled for throwing

food before. I touched my hair, still a little greasy from the mayonnaise, as we got into Gloria's car. Neither of us even bothered picking up the napkins and smocks on our seats.

"I just don't understand how this could happen," Mom went on. "You're lucky Gloria didn't have to work until one today. I had to ask if I could borrow her car, and I know the whole trailer park heard when I said I needed it because you'd gotten into a food fight. I don't even want to show my face around there anymore."

It was getting harder and harder for me to keep my mouth shut. I just couldn't believe she was lecturing me, when she'd been lying to me my whole life. She was even doing it now. She never had to ask Gloria if she could borrow the car; Gloria just gave it to her. The more I looked at her, the madder I got, so I turned my head to look out the window and saw Denny and his mom walking to their own car.

She'd never lied to *him*. I could tell by the way she guided him to their car with her hand on his shoulder. Denny had grown up knowing that Allie wasn't his full brother. Of course, that just made him hate Allie, and now it was making Winter hate me.

I thought maybe I could at least do something for Winter.

Mom was still talking as we pulled into the street, so I

made my voice loud enough to fill the whole car. "You said Winter could go to public school after summer ended."

"We're not talking about Winter right—"

"It's *November*!" I said, pointing out the window at the shiftless gray clouds that looked like they were on the verge of a downpour. "Maybe if you let Winter back into public school, she wouldn't have so many problems!"

"We're talking about you, Star. What I decide for Winter is none of your business anyway. Besides, you don't know the whole story. You don't know your sister as well as you think you do, and you know nothing about high school. So I think, out of the two of us, I'm the better judge of what's best for her!

"Now, whatever reason you had to throw food at that boy, I'm sure there was a better way you could have resolved it."

I said nothing, only crossed my arms hard against my chest.

"Well?" Mom asked. "Was there a better way you could have resolved it?"

Maybe it was because pouring that chocolate milk over Denny's head had felt so good, but I couldn't hold back anymore. I needed to say something horrible and mean, so I took Mom's words and turned them around on her. "It's none of your business. You don't know what's best for *me*, and you don't know Denny at all. So, out of the two of us, I'm the better judge of whether I should have thrown food at him!"

I waited for her to yell back. When she didn't, I turned away from the window to see why. Tears trailed down her cheeks from under her glasses.

And I thought, *So what?* She didn't know how much I'd cried because of her. But listening to her breathing through her mouth as she turned up the radio and rolled down the window, almost made me want to apologize, or maybe give her a hug.

Which made me hate her even more.

She was still crying when we pulled into Treasure Trailers. She stopped right at the entrance and got out of the car, and I glanced over at the tinfoil man's trailer. No movement, and the jack-o'-lantern was gone.

Mom didn't get back into the car, and it was running, and Gloria hated that, I knew, because it wasted gas. I looked around for her and found her standing in front of the mailboxes, staring down at some letters in her—

I jumped out of the car, flew over, and grabbed the whole stack from her hands.

There, on the top envelope, was my name.

CHAPTER 44

Mom hadn't shrunk at all, but when she spoke, I could tell she was angrier than ever before. *"What is that?"*

I ran. All the way into the trailer. Where I locked myself in the bathroom. As I ripped open the letter, my hands shaking, Mom's fist hammered against the door. *"Star, you get out here this instant!"*

There was one piece of paper inside the envelope, folded neatly down the middle, just like mine had been. Heart pounding, I unfolded it and read the first line. *Dear Dad.*

And stopped.

And read again. *Dear Dad, This is your daughter, Star Mackie. I'm ten years old now, and in fifth grade.*

That was my handwriting, not Dad's. This was my letter, the one I'd sent out last Monday. I threw it down on the bathroom floor and picked up the envelope from my lap, seeing what I should have seen the second I pulled it out of Mom's hands.

It was my envelope. The address in the center was Dad's. I had just been too excited to notice. Stamped across the bottom in big red letters was RETURN TO SENDER along with REASON: REFUSED.

Mom kept yelling and banging. "Star! Come out right now!"

What did that mean, REFUSED? I knew what *refused* meant, but what did RETURN TO SENDER, in red, in all capital letters, on an envelope that was supposed to go to my dad, mean?

"Star, please open the door." Mom's voice was quieter, and I could tell she had started crying again. "Tell me where that letter came from."

"Tell me what it means," I said, and I slid the envelope under the door for her. Mom would know. She knew about all that post office stuff. She knew that people actually did work there on Sundays, even though everyone thought the postal service was completely shut down for the day.

"What is it?" Mom asked.

"A letter to my dad," I said. "My *real* dad."

"And how did you figure that out?"

"It was on my birth certificate."

She cursed. As much as she hated Robert, I'd never heard her curse about him.

"Tell me what the 'Return to Sender' means!" I said.

"Well, that's obvious," Mom said. The trailer shifted and creaked, and through the crack under the door, I saw her sit down. "When people return something, usually it's because the addressee doesn't live there anymore."

My heart swelled with hope that set the Ferris wheel spinning again.

"But in this case, Frankie, or maybe his parents, took it to the post office and refused it. Sent it back, unopened. It means he didn't want this letter, Star." She paused. "And I could have told you that."

"You never told me anything!" I sank onto the cold toilet seat with my head in my hands, the Ferris wheel slowing to a complete stop. "You lied to me, my whole life. I always thought Dad just didn't care about me, that he loved Winter more. And you let me believe it! Does Frankie even know who I am?"

"Of course he does, Star," Mom said. "I thought he'd be different from Robert, but he turned out to be even more of a deadbeat."

"Robert's not a deadbeat. He sent Winter a birthday

card, and you were the one who wouldn't let him talk to her, and—"

"It's easier this way, Star," Mom said, and I could hear the anger snaking into her voice, could practically hear her shrinking down.

"Easier for *you*!" I shouted back. "What about *us*? What about Winter and me?"

For a few moments, Mom was quiet. Then she said, "Maybe you're right, Star. Maybe it was just easier for me. But just because Robert sent one birthday card doesn't mean he knows how to be a father."

"But what about the truck?" I said. "He gave her—"

"He gave her a truck that was going to the junkyard anyway," Mom said. "I tried to talk him out of it. This was back when we were still on speaking terms, before his wife was in the picture and making things even worse."

In my head, I listed all the things about the pickup that didn't work. Passenger's-side door, radio, air conditioner, heater, window crank, fifth gear. Broken side mirror. How loud it was. Were cars supposed to be that loud? Gloria's wasn't.

"Sometimes I'd ask him for help," Mom went on. "This was before you were born. Anyway, he'd never call me back, but a few days later there'd be a check in the mailbox. That's the kind of father Robert is, Star. The kind who throws money at problems until they go away."

He had given Winter money after she told him she was pregnant. It was weird, now that I think about it; parents are supposed to be mad when that kind of thing happens, but Robert hadn't seemed even the tiniest bit upset.

Did he even care about what happened to Winter?

"What about my dad?" I asked. "What about Frankie?"

"Well, he was a lot like Robert, actually," Mom said. "Except it was his parents who wrote the checks. He was young, younger than me. He didn't have his own money yet. Probably still doesn't. That's his parents' address here," she added, sliding the envelope back under the door. "It could have been them that refused it. They didn't like me very much. It has nothing to do with you. They just couldn't live with the fact that their spoiled little boy had knocked up some white-trash girl who already had a kid."

I picked up the envelope. It felt like nothing in my hands. Because it *was* nothing. I still didn't know who he was, really. "Tell me something good about him."

She was silent for so long, I was afraid there wouldn't be anything at all, but finally she said, "We took a poetry class together, at the community college. He really liked it, and he was good at it. Sometimes he wrote his own poems. He said they weren't very good, but he wrote one for me once, and I used to carry it around with me. Not anymore," she added, quickly. "I shredded it years ago."

I nodded, even though she couldn't see.

"I can't believe you figured it out," she said. "I was so careful. And if it makes you feel better, I wasn't just lying to you. I was lying to myself. It's easier to pretend that you're both Robert's than it is to admit that I got pregnant twice by two different guys who didn't care about anyone but themselves. Anyway, I am sorry."

"Sorry that I found out?"

"Sorry that I screwed up," she said. "Sorry that I let Winter know who her dad was, but not you. If you really want to, someday, I'll take you to meet him, Star. I owe you that much, at least."

But I didn't want to meet him. Things had gone so horribly wrong with Robert, and the fact that I was holding a REFUSED envelope in my hands told me that things weren't going to go so well with Frankie either.

But I still wanted *something*.

The phone rang, and Mom got up to answer it. I decided I'd been in the bathroom long enough, and anyway, my bed was a lot comfier than the toilet. Besides, even though I was trying, I couldn't stay mad at Mom anymore. In a way, I was hoping she'd lied to me again, but I knew this time she was telling me the truth.

"Hello?" Mom said into the phone. "Yes, this is her . . . Really? No, that's a surprise to me, too . . . Of course I will. Thank you so much." She hung up the phone, then stood over the sink for a few moments. "Why is it that you and your sister are so in sync these days?" she asked me. "That was Sarah Borne. Apparently Winter forged a note to get out of school today."

CHAPTER 45

Winter didn't get home until about 5:00, while Mom was picking up Gloria from work. Her truck rattled into the driveway, and as soon as she came in the door, I told her, "Mom knows you cut school today."

She had one arm out of her coat already but left the other one in. "You told her?"

"The school called."

"She wasn't out with Gloria?"

I hadn't thought it was actually my fault, Mom finding out; I just wanted to warn Winter. "I got into a fight at school," I said, without looking at her. "They called Mom and sent me home early." I almost told her about the returned letter, but I hadn't ever told her that I'd sent it in the first place, and I didn't feel like explaining.

"Who'd you get into a fight with?" she asked.

"Denny Libra," I said, quietly.

She froze. Except for her face, which began to frown, pulling her eyes and her eyebrows with it. "Did he . . . say anything? About me?"

I didn't want Winter to know what Denny had said, but I did want to ask her something. "Why did you want to get back together with Allie? Is he the father of your baby?"

Winter sank down at the built-in table, nodding. "I don't want to get back together with him, but I don't know what else to do."

I couldn't believe she was actually talking to me. I stayed quiet, knowing that if I said the wrong thing, she could be gone again.

"I'm tired of this," she said. "I don't know what I'm doing, but I don't want to keep it a secret anymore."

I reached over and took her hand. "Everything will get better soon," I said, hoping it was true.

Then footsteps crunched across the gravel and up the steps, and the door swung open, revealing Mom and Gloria. It was one of the few times I'd seen Gloria without a single donut.

"Oh, Winter's here," Gloria said. "I think I'll go back to

my trailer. This might be a good time to dump that microwave into the bay."

But Mom grabbed Gloria's arm and said, "Stay for a minute." The two of them stepped inside, and the door clicked closed behind them. "So," Mom said to Winter, "you gonna tell me where you were today?"

I tried to think of a good lie Winter could give, a good excuse for why she wasn't at school. But Winter must have decided that she was tired of keeping such a huge secret. "I saw a doctor."

"You went to a doctor?" Mom looked like she wanted to laugh. "After you refused to see one when you were actually sick, you decided to see a doctor now?" And then, just like that, the laughter was gone, and she said, "You're not sick, are you?"

"No," Winter said, her hand cradling her forehead. "I'm pregnant."

Mom didn't shrink at all. Her whole body was frozen, so I don't think she could have shrunk even if she wanted to. "No," Mom said. "You can't be serious. How could this happen?"

"Well, it happened to you, didn't it?" Winter said.

And still, Mom didn't shrink an inch. I couldn't believe she wasn't screaming. Maybe she'd used all her screaming energy on me.

"Well, I think it's time for me to go," Gloria said. "Come on, Star. Let's leave for a bit."

She didn't say where we were going, but I didn't want to go. I wanted to stay and make sure Winter would be all right. But Winter pulled me out of the table and gave me a little shove in Gloria's direction, so we left her and Mom staring at each other from across the linoleum.

"How mad do you think Mom's gonna be?" I asked Gloria as we made our way to the car.

Gloria shook her head. "Never would have thought this would happen to Winter, too. That sure is something." She unlocked the passenger's-side door for me and said, "Don't worry about Winter, though, sweetie. She'll be fine. Your mom's just upset because Winter turned out to be more like her than she wanted. I think she hoped the both of you would grow up without all the hardships she went through. But she'd love you no matter what. And so would I." We got in the car, and she rubbed the top of my hair.

"Gloria," I said, "did you give me a mullet?"

"It's a layered cut," she said automatically. But after peering critically at it for a moment, she added, "It was my first layered cut, though, so maybe it didn't turn out quite right. You want me to even it out for you?"

"Maybe," I said. I didn't think it would stop the teasing.

If I didn't have a mullet, they'd all just find something else to make fun of. Besides, I liked my mullet for now. "Maybe next year."

She clapped her hands together, grinning. "Great! What do you say we go rent a movie? You ever seen *A League of Their Own*?"

The library was closed, but Gloria said she'd splurge on a rental. We were the only two customers in the movie store, and while Gloria browsed the new-releases section, I checked out the candy displays. Next to a wall of chocolate bars was a spinning rack of postcards.

"Hey, Gloria," I yelled. I didn't think the woman working behind the register would mind the noise, since it was just us. "If you mail someone a postcard, can they send it back?"

"Not unless your address is on there," Gloria called out. "Can't send something back without a return address, you know."

Just what I'd been hoping. I spun the rack around and around, looking for a postcard that would not look like it came from California. No redwoods, and no giant Paul Bunyan statue either. Dad—Frankie—had to read it before he knew who it was from.

The one I picked out had *Attack of the 50 Ft. Woman* written on it, along with a fifty-foot woman attacking people. I raced up just as the woman behind the counter was telling Gloria the total. "This too, please."

"You writing to someone?" Gloria asked. "Someone back in Oregon?"

"Yup," I said. I just had to figure out what I'd write. I'd probably only get one chance, because then, after that, he'd just throw every postcard with my handwriting on it away.

By the time we got back to the trailer, Mom and Winter were done with their discussion, or argument, or whatever had happened. And nothing was broken. Mom said it was thanks to me, because if I hadn't made her feel like such a horrible mother—a horrible, lying, selfish mother—she would have hit the roof. Instead, they both sat on the fold-out couch, wrapped up in a quilt.

It was the closest I'd ever seen them.

Maybe it was because Mom knew how Winter was feeling, or maybe it was the other way around. But it was the first time Winter seemed happy to have Mom there.

"I got two movies," Gloria said, and she held them up. Mom pointed to one, and Winter pointed to the other.

"Oh, come on, Winter," Mom said. "It's a classic."

"It's in black and white, and it looks totally boring."

"Me and Gloria used to watch it all the time."

"Gloria and *I*, Mom."

"You know what I meant."

We didn't end up seeing either movie, because Mom and Winter spent the rest of the night arguing over which one to watch. It was a silly thing to argue about, but I guess they had to argue about *something*.

CHAPTER 46

Winter offered me a ride to school the next day, which I of course accepted, since it meant I wouldn't have to *traverse* the whole twelve blocks on foot. And also because I wanted to know what Mom and Winter had said to each other the night before, after I'd gone to bed.

"It was weird," Winter said, as we buckled our seat belts. "Mom said that it was my decision and that she supported me no matter what."

"So what are you going to do?" I asked.

"I still don't know. Isn't that terrible?" She took a sharp turn onto the next street, which nearly threw me against the window. "But I'm feeling a lot better about it now.

Mom says I should tell Allie, so I'll probably do that soon. I mean, I don't really care what he thinks, but maybe . . . I don't know. I guess I could see him being a good dad. We'll see."

We pulled up to the school a minute later. Winter turned into the parking lot instead of just dropping me off, and when she found a spot, she turned off the truck. "We're early," she said. "I wanted to tell you I'm sorry for being so mean lately. I was just freaking out, and I didn't want to deal with anything else." Her hand reached across the middle seat and grabbed mine. "I wonder if that's how our dads felt."

"They didn't want to deal with us?" I said.

"I didn't understand until we went to his house," Winter said, "but Robert really isn't that great. And I remember, when I was little, how everything was always on his terms. One day he suddenly decides he wants to see me at the fair. Or then he decides he wants to send me a birthday card. But you know what? I bet if I'd written him back, he wouldn't have answered. It's a good thing I was too scared to write to him and tell him I was going to visit," she added. "Otherwise he might not have been there. Although maybe that would have been better."

But if we'd never talked to Robert, I wouldn't know who *my* real dad was. And even though he'd refused my letter,

I wanted to get through to him anyway. I wanted him to know that even if he wasn't thinking about me, I was still here. I told Winter that, and I showed her the postcard with *Dear Frankie* written on it and nothing else. I hadn't decided what to write yet.

"But I'll figure it out myself," I said. Whatever I ended up writing, I didn't want it to come from Winter. It had to come from me.

"If you insist," Winter said, just as the bell rang. I started to move out of the truck, but Winter held my hand tightly. "You have any other problems you need help with?" she asked. "I want to make it up to you."

There were so many. Denny was always going to be a problem, I figured. People were still calling me Star Trashy, and Langston liked me, whatever that meant. And of course, the biggest problem of all: I still had no club.

But I did have hope. It had started spinning again after I'd talked to Mom. And maybe it was stupid to think so, but hope was telling me that things really were going to be okay.

"Don't worry about me," I told Winter. "Are you going to be okay?" I asked as she leaned over to hug me good-bye. "I was afraid it was because we're half sisters," I whispered into her hair. "That that's why you wouldn't talk to me anymore. Because you didn't like me anymore."

"Yeah, right," she whispered back.

I waved as she pulled out of the parking lot. And then I kind of wished I had asked her for help, because maybe, just maybe, everything wasn't going to be okay.

But I willed that Ferris wheel to keep on moving by putting one foot in front of the other until I finally got to class.

CHAPTER 47

Mr. Savage switched our seats. I figured maybe he was tired of alphabetical seating, but Jared told me it was because Denny and I couldn't sit near each other anymore.

Good, I thought. But bad, too, because Genny also sat far away and wouldn't look at me, all through class. Instead, she paid extra attention to everything Mr. Savage said and tugged her sleeves down to her wrists. If I'd known that Genny was going to be this upset, I never would have thrown anything at Denny.

During math, Mr. Savage got a phone call. It lasted all of two seconds before he put his hand over the receiver and said, "Denny. Star. Office."

Somewhere between my new desk and the door I remembered that I was supposed to write a letter of apology to Denny *and I totally forgot*! Why couldn't Mom have called the school to say, "Oh, you know, last night I found out my older daughter is pregnant, and I told Star the truth about her deadbeat father. Could you give her an extra day on that apology?" But I wasn't mad at Mom, because she was probably just a little distracted.

So I arrived at the office empty-handed.

Denny had about a dozen pieces of paper in his hand, some crumpled, and I was a little flattered that he'd written me such a long apology, but then he told the principal, "I want to say mine out loud."

The principal probably thought the same thing I did about Denny's apology being so many pages, because he checked his watch and said, "Well . . ."

Denny plowed on ahead and said, "I'm sorry I called you and your sister trashy and for telling you not to be around my sister." And he said it while looking me in the eye. And he even said it without glaring.

Denny Libra.

A satisfied smile took up the lower half of the principal's face. He obviously did not realize how un-Denny-like this was.

"I'd like to say my apology out loud, too," I said. I looked

Denny in the eye and tried not to glare. If Denny could say an apology, so could I. "I'm sorry I called you a termite and dumped milk on you. And . . ." I almost didn't want to say it, but I knew I had to. "I'm sorry I kicked you out of the club. You can be in the club again, if you want."

Denny nodded, and the principal clapped his hands together and said that he could tell we really meant it and that we'd both have detention this week but that he hoped we could put this behind us and try to get along.

Neither of us rolled our eyes.

Outside the principal's office, before I took one step in the direction of Mr. Savage's room, Denny shoved his twelve crumpled-and-smoothed pages at me with a rough-sounding "Here."

Some of the papers were stained, but I recognized them right away, because at the top of the very first page in my handwriting were the words *Week 1 Vocabulary Sentences.*

"Heavenly Donuts!" I said, flipping through the whole stack. "Where did you get my sentences?"

"Out of the trash," Denny said, as if I were stupid and he hadn't apologized for a single thing. His voice softened when he added, "You kept throwing them away, so you obviously didn't want them anymore."

Denny's name had popped up a few times in my sentences, I knew, so I asked, "Did you read them?" When he didn't answer, I knew he had. Great. Just what else had I written in there?

"Look," said Denny, "I'm giving them back so you can turn them in and get your stupid club started again." He paused while I gaped at him. "Genny won't talk to me," he said, looking at the floor. "She's never been this upset. When we got home yesterday, she scrubbed all her tattoos off. Then she cried in her room for the rest of the day. Mom had to drag her out of bed this morning, and she screamed all the way down the stairs."

Of course Denny had a house with stairs.

"Isn't that what you wanted?" I shot, because he had. And I wanted to rub it in. "For her to be *normal*? For her to *not be like me*?" And then I felt horrible, because Denny actually looked upset about it. As much as Denny disliked his half brother, he really loved his sister.

"I want her to be happy," he said. "So get your dumb club back. And don't let her get detention anymore." He began shuffling his way back to class.

"Hey," I said. "Thanks."

"Whatever," he said, without looking back.

What a jerk. "I regret letting you back in the club!" I called to him.

"And I regret having to be in it," he said.

I figured that was the best we could do.

CHAPTER 48

We came back just before recess. I knew Mr. Savage would keep me inside, and I knew he had a bucket of water with my name on it. The desks weren't even slightly dirty anymore, since I'd been washing them every day, so I don't know why he kept making me do it. Didn't he have anything else that needed to be cleaned?

The bell rang, and Mr. Savage told me to stay in, and when everyone had left the room, I gritted my teeth, clenched my toes inside my combat boots, smoothed my hair, and marched up to his desk, where I dropped my whole pile of crumpled-and-smoothed sentences right on top of the papers he was grading.

Then I had to concentrate on standing and not falling over or running to the other side of the room.

Mr. Savage picked up the first page of my sentences, put it down, leafed through the whole pile, scratched his beard, and told me, "You can go to recess, then."

"Do I get my club back?" I practically shouted, causing him to scoot his chair away from me.

"Let me look them over first."

So I forced myself to walk, not run, out of the classroom, and when I finally got out into the open air, my fists managed to unclench themselves, and my toes straightened out, and my jaw relaxed. It was too soon to tell if I would get my club back or not, and I didn't want to get Genny's hopes up, so I sat down on the bench by the map of the United States, kicking a couple of pebbles at California.

I took out my postcard. *Dear Frankie* stared back up at me. What in the world was I supposed to write next? All I knew about him—all Mom had told me—was that he liked poetry. And I thought that anyone who liked poetry couldn't be a complete deadbeat jerk.

Besides, I didn't know any poems. Only Emily Dickinson ones. Did he even like Emily Dickinson? It was worth a shot. I wrote, *"Hope is . . ."* and stopped.

He had written Mom a poem.

Maybe I should write him one.

But then the bell rang, and then we had science. It was a journaling day, so we were writing about the progress of our sprouting lima beans. *November is a terrible time to sprout beans,* I wrote. Halfway through, Denny and I looked at each other from across the room without glaring. I think he was trying to ask if I'd turned in the sentences, so I nodded and went back to my dying bean.

When the lunch bell rang, Mr. Savage told me to stay while the rest of the class went off to the cafeteria. I inched toward the front of the room, unable to make myself get there any quicker. But eventually there I was, gripping the edge of Mr. Savage's desk for support.

"I'm glad you turned these in," he started. "I'm curious about why some of these sentences are about what a terrible teacher you think I am."

Oh, right. I hadn't only written bad things about Denny. I'd written some bad things about Mr. Savage, too. Maybe I should have reread those sentences before I turned them in. I told Mr. Savage how the sentences were written a long time ago and that I never thought anyone would see them.

"Hmm." He had the whole pile of sentences in front of him, his fingers lifting the corners and letting them fall back down. "So you don't feel that way anymore, then?"

I could have lied and said yes, because even though I

didn't like him, I never wanted to hurt Mr. Savage's feelings. But I looked him in the eye and said, "Well, you did think I hadn't done my sentences when I really had. And it's not fair to treat me like a delinquent just because I wasn't turning in the sentences." I figured I'd share one good thing about him, so I added, "I liked learning about Emily Dickinson."

"I know," he said. "Miss Fergusson was telling me all about your club the other day. Trying to convince me to let you keep doing it. She said you were very respectful and smart, and I just kept thinking, 'Are we talking about the same Star Mackie?'" He laughed, although I didn't think it was very funny. "Anyway, when I read your sentences, I realized she was right. I just had a hard time seeing it."

"I guess you're not so bad either," I said, which made him laugh again. He had a weird sense of humor, I decided.

He took the first four pages off the pile and slid them over to me, saying, "I do need these first ones redone, unless you're willing to accept half credit on them. You're supposed to—"

"Use the words in a sentence," I finished for him. "That's why I never turned them in." The ticking clock reminded me that I was supposed to be in the cafeteria, and that the line for hot lunch would be very long, and that I would soon not have enough time to talk to Genny. "Do I get my club back now?"

It was like he knew I was in a hurry, so he took a long time thinking about it. "Are you still going to have it in Miss Fergusson's room? Because if you wanted, you could have it here again. I know a lot about Emily Dickinson, you know."

The clock kept ticking, but I knew I wasn't getting out of there without a good answer, so I ignored it. "Yeah, I know. But I think we might actually change the club now. And I'm probably not going to be in charge of it anymore. We'd probably have to take a vote, and Miss Fergusson has a quilt and a couch, and that's a major plus."

"That's too bad," he said. "Miss Fergusson tells me it's a great club. But if you ever want any help, you know, with the Emily Dickinson stuff . . ."

I nodded, taking my Week 1 sentences. "I'll give these back to you soon." And I turned to leave, finally.

"One more thing," he said. "Do you really hate the weird words?"

I stopped, confused. "What?"

"I'm required to teach you certain words," he said. "But I can't resist some great old-fashioned ones, too. I know they'll never show up on tests, but I keep hoping I'll hear someone using them."

I always assumed Mr. Savage was trying to torture us with those weird words, not that he really liked them. "Well," I told him, "I've been using the word *vexation* a lot. I guess it's not that old-fashioned."

I tried to leave again, but before I made it out the door, I heard, "One more thing."

"You *already said that,*" I told him.

He laughed again. It was more of a chuckle. "Don't get into any more fights, all right? It makes me look bad."

"The beard makes you look bad," I told him, and I was gone before he could think of *one more thing.*

CHAPTER 49

I ran all the way to the cafeteria, even though you're not supposed to run in the hallways. The hot-lunch line was too long, so I skipped it. Who needs to eat, anyway? I found Denny and Genny sitting across from each other, completely silent except, probably, for their chewing.

"Hi, Denny," I said first, to show Genny that there were no hard feelings about Denny being a jerk all year and the big fight we'd had yesterday.

I think he caught on to what I was doing, because he said, in a very fake, happy voice, "Oh, hi, Star!" Which was the first time he'd actually said my name. To my face, at least.

But I think Genny could tell we were faking. "I'm sorry

Denny was such a crab to you," she told me. "I understand if you don't want to be my friend anymore."

"I'm sorry, too," I told her. "For making your brother look like a doofus."

Denny was back to glaring.

"He always looks like a doofus," Genny said, and Denny shifted his glare to her. It was nice to hear her standing up to him a little. "Do you have anything to eat?" she asked me, and before I could answer, she ripped her sandwich in two and gave me a piece.

And I knew, even though she wasn't giving anyone the elbow, that this was what it was like to have a best friend. So I told her thanks and explained, while she made a neat pile of salami on the table, that I'd gotten the club back. "It'll probably just be called the Poetry Club now," I told her. "We'll do other people besides Emily Dickinson. Maybe even some haikus."

"Oh, good!" she said. "Let's make sure Langston stops drawing bras all the time, though. And, Denny, you have to talk more."

"Fine," Denny muttered.

"What?" Genny said, holding her ear closer to him.

"Fine, I will talk more, and in complete sentences," he said, glaring at me. I guess that wasn't going to change.

"Do you still want me to find some more club members?" Genny asked. I remembered what Denny had said about keeping her out of detention.

"No," I told her. "I think the club is perfect just the way it is."

"We're exclusive!" Genny shouted. She turned to another lunch table and tapped a fifth-grade boy on the shoulder. When he turned around, she yelled, "YOU CAN'T JOIN THE CLUB!"

I wouldn't trade Genny for all the fifth-graders in Mr. Savage's class. It turns out I just needed one person.

One friend.

A friend who didn't care that I lived at Treasure Trailers and who thought my mullet was cool.

And I had three, if I counted Eddie and Langston. I didn't know how they felt about the mullet, or Treasure Trailers, but they were definitely friends. If they weren't, I probably would have been punched by now.

I looked at Denny and sighed. If I had to put up with him to be Genny's friend, then I guess it was worth it.

Genny and I spent the rest of the day telling everyone they weren't in the club. Some people said, "What club?" and some people said, "Who are you?" and most people said, "Who cares?"

But we kept doing it anyway.

Star Mackie

November 5

Week 1 Vocabulary Sentences

When I first sat behind lanky Denny Libra, I had no idea I'd end up being best friends with his sister, or that I'd end up throwing applesauce at his head. I was too busy thinking that living in poverty would keep me from making any friends at all. But now I have an abundance of friends, all thanks to the Emily Dickinson Club. (And you, I guess, Mr. Savage. For writing her poems on the board.)

But now the club's changing, and Eddie's going to make us read a bunch of alternative poems so we aren't just reading about Emily Dickinson all the time. I was a little reluctant to change the club, but it turns out there are a few other good poets, and besides, it's a lot harder to run a club than I thought it would be. I'd rather let Eddie run it sometimes than get hysterical every week trying to find something new and interesting to do.

Now I am trying to make sure these sentences are complete and circumstantial (even if they're not alphabetical), but I am also occasionally looking at the mostly blank postcard sitting next to me. It's supposed to be for my dad, who is not even neutral about wanting to see me—he is completely opposed to seeing me at all, ever. But he can't send back a covert poem that is cleverly disguised as a postcard.

So I'm sorry to tell you that I think, after this, I am done with the word vexation.

Hopefully forever.

CHAPTER 50

I found Eddie in Miss Fergusson's room after school, scowling at a pile of papers. "I can't believe you're making me do this," he said as I approached his desk.

"I thought 'The Turtle and the Bagpipe' was your favorite poem," I said.

"It's 'The Bagpipe Who Didn't Say No,'" he said, "and I told you, it's not my favorite. I just couldn't memorize any of the poems in that book, and I wanted to keep it so badly." He told me how he'd snuck the book from Mrs. Flower's desk, written the poem in there, and then recited it for her the next day. And then she'd had to give him the book, because the poem was in there, after all.

I can't believe he didn't think he was smart.

But I could tell it really was his favorite, still, because he'd never found another poem to take its place as *Amarica's Gratist Poem*. "Besides," I told him, "I want to know why you like it so much."

"Whatever," he said. "What metaphors are we supposed to pull from here, anyway? And what are we gonna talk about? It's a love poem about a turtle and a bagpipe." He brushed all the papers into his backpack and, waving good-bye to Miss Fergusson, headed to the door. I headed out with him.

Once we were in the hallway, I handed him my postcard. "Read this and tell me what you think."

"Who's Frankie?" he asked.

"My dad."

"Why do you call him Frankie? I don't call my dad by his first name."

"It's a long story. Will you shut up and read it already?"

He shoved me, just a little bit, but stopped to read. I watched his eyes move back and forth, reading the poem I'd written on there. The same one I'd started last month. I'd finally finished it.

Hope is a Ferris wheel –
It takes you Low and High;
And when you reach the Top,

It's like you can touch The Sky!
And when it takes you Down –
Hope becomes A Thing
That, When you're getting Off,
You take With you to Bring.

"Your meter's off a bit," Eddie said, handing back the postcard. I didn't know what that meant. "But it's good," he added, thankfully, because I wasn't going to send this to Dad without Eddie the poetry genius's approval.

I tucked it safely away in my pocket.

On my way home, I stopped by the mailbox, hoping, really hoping, that Dad would like the poem so much, he wouldn't throw it away or rip it to shreds or anything like that.

The thing was, I would never know. Because he couldn't send back the postcard, and until I decided to send him my address, he also couldn't write me back at all.

I knew that when he read it, he probably wouldn't understand it. Maybe he'd never been on a Ferris wheel before, and there was no way he'd know that I'd been on one. But I still wanted to share my poem with him, because I had figured out how to finish it all on my own. I knew he liked poetry, and if Eddie said it was a good poem, then

I knew Frankie would think so, too, even if he found it confusing.

Besides, it was the best kind of poem: a truth poem. That, I decided, was the fourth Emily Dickinson category. For her, hope was a thing with feathers, and for me, it's a Ferris wheel. And I hope it never stops spinning.

Anyway, I dropped the postcard in. Because the postcard itself wasn't a hope; it was a dream. And dreams need to fly.

Acknowledgments

There is only one name on the front of this book, but don't be fooled. Without the help of some very generous people (and institutions), this book simply wouldn't exist.

First, thanks to my family—Mom, Jessica, and Donald—for practically everything. Support, food, shelter, advice, socks, phone calls, and most importantly, a sense a humor.

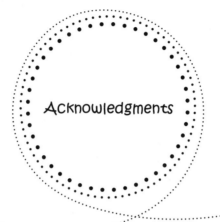

The Vermont College of Fine Arts is an amazing place, and I am so very proud to have been a part of it. I would like to extend extra thanks to my four advisors: Alan Cumyn, Rita Williams-Garcia, Julie Larios, and Shelley Tanaka, all of whom were instrumental in Star's development. And another thank-you to my graduating class, the Thunder Badgers, for being collectively awesome and awe-inspiring.

Elysia Willis and Brian Millet were my first (non-VCFA) readers, and it's because of them that I didn't lose sight of this story. (And that I survived my first year of graduate school.)

Speaking of graduate school, I never would have made it there if I hadn't taken Professor Kathryn Reiss's YA literature and writing classes in college.

And speaking of teachers, my former drama teacher, Barry Blake, was kind enough to read my first draft and give me extensive notes. (He was also kind enough to put up with me in high school.)

All of these people helped me to be a better writer.

Then there's Sara Crowe. As an agent, she's unstoppable. She never gave up on me or my book, and I'm so happy I've got her in my corner.

Tamar Brazis, my editor, took this book and made it shine. It's because of her that I am proud to put my name on it. And to the rest of the Amulet team (and especially the three M's: Maggie, Melissa, and Maria) for being the best publisher a writer could ask for.

And finally, there's Brandon. He consoled me through rejections, never complained about reading a draft before

I sent it off to Sara or Tamar, and bought me countless candy bars when I needed them. Thanks for sticking around, buddy.

About the Author

ROBIN HERRERA is an aspiring cat lady living in Portland, Oregon, with her fiancé and one very mean (but precious) cat. She received her BA from Mills College and her MFA in writing for children and young adults from Vermont College of Fine Arts. When not chasing cats, she can be found at her desk at Oni Press, where she works as an administrative assistant, or at the library, where she severely abuses the hold system. This is her first book.

HOPE IS A FERRIS WHEEL

READER'S GROUP GUIDE

1. Sometimes Star's idea of normal doesn't match up with other people's perceptions. What are some aspects of her appearance or life that Star sees one way but other people see a different way?

2. When Star starts the Trailer Park Club, why do you think she has a hard time finding other members to join? Was there ever a time when you judged someone without knowing them?

3. How does the author use Star's vocabulary lists to tell you more about Star and her life? Why do you think Star doesn't turn them in, even after she learns how to do them correctly?

4. Star objects to vocabulary words that she considers old-fashioned—like *defenestrate* and *vexation*—because the same thing can be said in a more modern way. Do you think it's important to preserve words, or should language be allowed to change over time?

5. Star collects a group of friends she didn't mean to when she starts the Emily Dickinson Club. How do they—Genny, Eddie, and Langston—express their friendship to her? What does friendship mean to you?

6. The first time Star saw the man she thought was her father, she was riding the Ferris wheel at the fair. How does the physical experience of being on a Ferris wheel relate to their relationship? How does Star use it as a metaphor?

7. Star thinks Emily Dickinson, who had a very sad life, was "writing to make herself happy," just like her sister, Winter. What are some of the reasons people write? Why does Star? Why do you?

8. Winter likes to write scary stories, but when her teachers read them, she got in trouble. Do you think the school was right to expel her over her words? Why or why not?

9. Star is inspired by Emily Dickinson's poem "Hope," also known as "Hope is the thing with feathers," and she discusses the idea of hope with many other characters in the book. Which character's definition of hope do you like best? How would you describe hope?

10. Gloria has been friends with Star's mother, Carly, since they were kids. Over the course of the book, Genny becomes Star's best friend. What are some similarities and differences between these two sets of best friends?

11. After going to Oregon with Winter, Star finds out that the man she thought was her father really isn't. How does Star think this discovery will change her relationships with Winter and her mother? Does she still think that after she talks to them about it?

12. Star writes a letter to her biological father, but it is returned unread. She then decides to send him a postcard with a poem she wrote, even though he might never read it. Why do you think she sent him her poem? Do you think this was a good idea? Why or why not?

13. Star's classmate Jared writes a poem based on Emily Dickinson's "I'm nobody! Who are you?" (page 86). Read the real poem below:

I'm nobody ! Who are you ?
Are you nobody, too ?
Then there's a pair of us — don't tell !
They'd banish us, you know.

How dreary to be somebody !
How public, like a frog
To tell your name the livelong day
To an admiring bog !

Star thinks all of Emily Dickinson's poems fit into a few themes: nature, God, death, and truth. Where does the above poem fit? Do you think there should be other categories? What does this poem mean to you? Would you rather be somebody or nobody?

14. Eddie wants the Emily Dickinson Club to begin with reading “Because I could not stop for Death,” also called “The Chariot” (page 101). Later, he recites a poem by Gwendolyn Brooks for Star (page 129). Compare and contrast Dickinson’s “Because I could not stop for Death” with Gwendolyn Brooks’s “We Real Cool.”

15. In her poem “A bird came down the walk” (or “In the Garden”), Emily Dickinson uses the word *plashless* to mean the same thing as *splashless,* though it has one letter missing.

A bird came down the walk :
He did not know I saw ;
He bit an angle-worm in halves
And ate the fellow, raw.

And then he drank a dew
From a convenient grass,
And then hopped sidewise to the wall
To let a beetle pass.

He glanced with rapid eyes
That hurried all abroad, —

They looked like frightened beads, I thought ;
He stirred his velvet head

Like one in danger ; cautious,
I offered him a crumb,
And he unrolled his feathers
And rowed him softer home

Than oars divide the ocean,
Too silver for a seam,
Or butterflies, off banks of noon,
Leap, plashless, as they swim.

Can you think of a word that you can shorten to make another word—one that either has the same meaning or means something completely different?

16. Eddie doesn't care for poems by Robert Frost. One of Frost's most well-known poems is "The Road Not Taken." How does this poem compare to some of Emily Dickinson's poems about nature?

17. When Eddie takes over the poetry club, they read the poem "Dreams" by Langston Hughes (page 175). Compare and contrast this poem with "Hope is the thing with feathers" (pages 81–82). What do you think is the difference between hopes and dreams?

18. Eddie's favorite poem used to be "The Bagpipe Who Didn't Say No," by Shel Silverstein. He never explains why it was his favorite. Why do you think he chose to memorize it? Do you think the poem is humorous, or do you think it's sad?

19. **SUGGESTED ACTIVITY:** Star writes a poem inspired by Emily Dickinson (pages 245–246), which makes use of the poet's signature style. Try writing your own poem—using dashes, capitalization, and exclamation points—on one of Dickinson's favorite topics: nature!

20. **SUGGESTED ACTIVITY:** Create your own vocabulary list, modeled after Star's homework, with ten words that mean something to you. Write one or two sentences that demonstrate the meaning of the word and that also communicate something about your life.

This book was designed by Maria T. Middleton. The text is set in 11-point Versailles, a typeface designed by Adrian Frutiger for Linotype in 1984. Inspiration for this sharp, triangular serif came from nineteenth-century metal type engravings found on the memorial of Charles Garnier, architect of the Paris Opera building. The display faces are Frontage Bold and Bulb. This book was printed and bound by RR Donnelley in Crawfordsville, Indiana. Its production was overseen by Kathy Lovisolo.